NEVER, AGAIN

NEVER, AGAIN

ENDRE FARKAS

For Geri
Best
Ever
Oct 19, 2016

Signature
EDITIONS

© 2016, Endre Farkas

Cover design by Doowah Design.
Photo of Endre Farkas by dhfoto.
Cover images from Creative Commons. Top: "A Soviet tank attempts to clear a road barricade in Budapest, Hungary." Bottom: "A destroyed T-34-85 tank at the Móricz Zsigmond Square."

Acknowledgements
I would like to thank: Carolyn Marie Souaid for lovingly pushing me to do it, and for her patient ears and eagle eyes; Odette Dubé for her early read and comments; and Katilina Kürtösi and Judit Molnár for their help with historical and cultural details.

Excerpt from *The Paul Street Boys* by Ferenc Molnár, translated by Louis Rittenberg, translation revised by George Szirtes. Published by Corvin Books, Hungary.

This book was printed on Ancient Forest Friendly paper.
Printed and bound in Canada by Hignell Book Printing Inc.

We acknowledge the support of the Canada Council for the Arts and the Manitoba Arts Council for our publishing program.

Library and Archives Canada Cataloguing in Publication

Farkas, Endre, 1948-, author
        Never, again / Endre Farkas.

Issued in print and electronic formats.
ISBN 978-1-927426-86-9 (paperback).
--ISBN 978-1-927426-87-6 (epub)

        1. Hungary--History--Revolution, 1956--Fiction. I. Title.

PS8561.A72N49 2016   C813'.54   C2016-904950-7
                                          C2016-904951-5

Signature Editions
P.O. Box 206, RPO Corydon, Winnipeg, Manitoba, R3M 3S7
www.signature-editions.com

To my parents, my children,
and to those who fought bravely for
freedom in the 1956 Hungarian Uprising

SEPTEMBER

·

1956

1

"Once upon a time, a long, long, long…"

"…time ago…"

"…oh so far, far, far…"

"…away…"

"…in the land of the Mighty Magyars, in the county of the bold Hajdús, in the beautiful village of Békes, lived a brave young boy. And this amazingly brave young boy, in the middle of the night, zig-zagged through his secret mazes to ride with the bold Hajdús into battles against the terrible Turks, manned with steely grip and gaze the turret machine-gun of his tank to heroically defend his motherland, wrestled with noble body and soul in titanic battles against the brutish Redshirts, hopped rumbling trains, swam raging rivers, climbed steep mountains and traversed treacherous prairies to see fantastic things. No enemy, terrain or monster was too big or too dangerous to stop Tomi Wolfstein."

"You forgot something, Papa."

"Ah. And Tomi Wolfstein, the most talented and famous soccer player ever known in Hungary, weaved and dribbled on the Golden Green to score brilliant goals for the best soccer team in the world."

Tomi gives his father a sleepy smile.

Sanyi kisses Tomi on the forehead and tucks the covers around him. "All you have to do is dream, my dear son. So close your eyes now and go to sleep."

—

Tomi's eyes are wide open. He wriggles along the inviting folds, curves and turns of the dark maze. As he feels its welcoming warmth, hears its soft breathing and tastes every lump-clump tickle of its wrinkles, more than ever, he senses the call of a new adventure.

His head hits something hard and he almost cries out. But he bites his lip and becomes statue-still. He mustn't make any noise. When the throbbing subsides, he pops his head out from under the duvet and grabs the bed's footboard. Slowly he turns his head to the left, to the right. He sees nothing. He stares ahead. He listens. He hears loud thumping. He hears loud waves. It's his heart. It's his breathing. He sighs.

As his eyes adjust to the darkness, he feels the sting of the crisp air on his skin and in his nostrils; the air feels so new that he's sure he is the first one to breathe it. He slithers over the edge of the bed and onto the terracotta floor. The night-chilled tiles make him want to yelp but he doesn't. He doesn't want to wake anyone. Biting his lip, again, he tiptoes to the door.

Often in the early early morning, he crawls in to snuggle between his mother and father. He likes the feeling of his parents' bodies on either side of him. It makes him feel safe, makes him feel that nothing can hurt him. It makes him want to stay in bed forever. But not today.

His parents always rise to the cock-a-doodle-doo of Red, even on Sundays, when they don't have to go to work. Tomi stays beneath the duvet cocooned in the warmth they leave behind, and listens to his mother and Emma-mama moving about in the kitchen, poking the ashes to rekindle the stove, while his father fetches water from the well and Dezsö-papa collects the eggs from the clucking hens. Usually, he stays in bed until breakfast is almost ready. When his father calls, he climbs out from beneath the duvet and tiptoes across the cold tile, yelping all the way. When he reaches his perch at the verandah table he shouts "Help! Help!"

"What's wrong? What's wrong?" his father always calls from the kitchen.

"I can't see. I can't see!"

"Oh no! Oh no! Why not? Why not?" he asks with exaggerated worry, as he brings Tomi his cup of warm milk.

"Because my eyes are closed!" And he pops his eyes wide open, smiles and reaches for the hand-warming cup.

"A miracle! A miracle!" his father always cries out, clapping his hands to his cheeks. "A miracle!"

—

But today is different. Today he wanted to be the first one up. It is the first Monday of September 1956. It's his first day of school. From now on, he'll be getting up earlier to learn to add, to subtract, memorize dates, recite poetry and play soccer on a field with real nets like the ones on the Golden Green. He is a big boy now.

He takes a deep breath, pushes slowly down on the handle and opens the door to the verandah just wide enough to squeeze through. Up on his morning perch, he leans against the cool stucco wall, feels its prickles through his pyjamas. The fresh morning breeze gives him goose bumps, and he wraps his arms about his legs, rests his chin on his knees and watches the ending of night.

The world is becoming visible. As a pink glow rises from the horizon, birds begin chirping and the morning yawns awake.

The yard is divided into two by a shoulder-high picket fence. Last year, it was head high. Emma-mama's vegetable garden and rose bushes are on the near side. She guards her roses like a mother hen her chicks. Every morning, she checks the roses for bugs, petal by petal. He has seen her bend over rose after rose, to peer into them. When she bends over to smell them, he imagines a giant bumblebee trying to get at the pollen inside the petals. And sometimes, when she bends really close, the tip of her nose gets smeared with yellowish-orange powder. When she straightens, eyes closed, she always has a big smile on her face. He has often wondered why. He has even heard her humming and talking to them.

Emma-mama also loves her vegetable garden, but she doesn't talk or hum to the vegetables. At least he's never heard her. Every spring since she and Dezsö-papa came to live with them, she has planted potatoes, and sowed carrot, pea and tomato seeds in neat straight rows. The first shoots always remind him of the straight lines of soldiers at May Day parades. All summer, Emma-mama keeps the garden neat by making him and Gabi weed. They squat-march up and down the rows, plucking weeds. He doesn't like that part, but when the vegetables are ready, he loves eating them, especially the carrots. When the carrots' green leaves sprout and are tall and proud, like Red's cockscomb, he loves to pull one up and bite into its crunchy sweetness.

—

"Once upon a time, a long, long, long, long…"

"…time ago," Tomi shouts whenever he thinks his father has gone on long enough.

"…there was an old farmer who was so poor he had to sell his skinny cow and skinny goose so that his family would not starve. It had been a long cold, cold, cold, cold, cold…"

"…winter…"

"…and he and his family had very little food left in the larder. The shelves were empty except for a small jar of plum butter, a small sack of flour, a small jar of dill pickles and a sliver of winter salami. In the root cellar there was only a wilting head of cabbage. Now it was spring, the time for planting, a time for hope. But all the old farmer had in the granary was one carrot seed that he had carefully put into a small clay jar last fall. He turned the jar upside down and spilled the tiny, tiny, tiny…"

"…seed…"

"…into his old, calloused, cracked palm. Carefully, he shuffled to the garden, where his wife, son, dog, cat and mouse were all waiting. He took his son's soft, soft, soft…"

"…hand…"

"…and placed the seed in his palm. The old farmer knelt down and poked a little hole into the earth.

"'Come,' he said to his son, 'and put the seed in the ground.' The boy knelt next to his father and dropped it into the hole. His mother knelt too and gently, the way she tucked her son in each night, covered it. Then the son filled his watering can and sprinkled the earth with cool, fresh well water.

"The mother, the father, the son, the dog, the cat and the mouse stood in a circle around the seed. 'Grow, my little seed, grow. Grow into a large fine carrot, grow. Grow, my little root, grow. Grow sweet, grow fat, grow big,' they recited like a prayer. And every morning, all spring and all summer, the poor farmer went to his garden to water the little mound and repeat his morning prayer, 'Grow, my little seed, grow. Grow into a large fine carrot, grow. Grow, my little root, grow. Grow sweet, grow fat and grow big.'

"Spring and summer came and went, but nothing grew. Not a single peek-a-boo shoot of a leaf. Not a hello-I'm-here. The old man was discouraged, but still every morning he watered it and prayed over it. One morning, on his way to the garden, he felt autumn's coolness on his cheeks and sniffed winter's breath. He was worried that there would be nothing for his family. He feared that he, his wife, child, dog, cat and mouse would starve. He wondered what he would do when, lo and behold, there, sticking out of the ground, as big as a gooseberry bush, was a huge leafy cockscomb carrot top. He could not believe his eyes! He rejoiced. Now his family would have enough to eat for the coming winter. He bent down and stroked its fresh green leaves. They were as wide as his palm. The stems were as thick as his wrist. He grabbed the carrot by its stem and pulled. And he pulled and he pulled. And he…"

"…grunted and grunted and grunted…"

"…and he…"

"…pulled and he pulled and pulled…"

"…but he could not pull the carrot out."

"He called his wife. 'Dear wife, come quickly and help. The carrot is so big that I cannot pull it out by myself.' His wife rushed out to him. She could not believe how big it was. 'Come, dear wife, help me pull it out.' She grabbed her husband by the waist and together they…"

"…pulled and they pulled and grunted and pulled but could not pull the carrot out…"

"…Then the farmer's wife called their son. 'Dear son, come and help us. The carrot is so big that we cannot pull it out.' The boy came and he could not believe it either. 'Come, dear son, help us pull it out.' The son grabbed his mother by the waist, who held her husband, and they…"

"…pulled and pulled and grunted and pulled, but could not pull the carrot out."

"'Dear dog,' the son called. 'Come and help us. The carrot is so big that we cannot pull it out.' The dog came and barked in disbelief. 'Come, dear dog, help us pull it out.' So the dog grabbed the boy by the waist, and they pulled and they…"

"…pulled and grunted and pulled, but could not pull the carrot out."

"'Dear cat,' the dog barked. 'Come and help. The carrot is so big that we cannot pull it out.' The cat came and meowed in disbelief. 'Come, dear cat, help us pull it out'. So the cat grabbed the dog by the tail, and they pulled and they…"

"…pulled and they pulled and grunted and pulled but could not pull the carrot out."

"'Dear mouse,' the cat meowed, 'come and help us. The carrot is so big that we cannot pull it out.' The mouse came and squeaked disbelief. 'Come, dear mouse, help us pull it out.' He grabbed the cat by the tail, and …

"…they pulled and they pulled and they all pulled and grunted and pulled…"

"And, all of a sudden, out popped the carrot! The father, the mother, the son, the dog, the cat and the mouse all tumbled backwards and fell to the ground. When they stood up and looked, they could not believe their eyes. 'A miracle! A miracle,' they shouted. It was the biggest carrot they had ever seen. It was so big that it almost filled up the garden. They laughed and danced around the giant carrot. It was so big that it took them almost the whole day to load it onto their wagon. It was so big that the wagon almost collapsed under the weight. It was so heavy that their skinny old mare could not pull it to market. So the father, the mother, the son, the dog, the cat and the mouse all helped push the wagon. When they finally arrived at the market, everyone gathered round to see this miracle. They could not believe it. A man from a travelling circus saw it and bought it. They sold it for a fortune and so had enough money to live like kings, happily, ever after."

Of course, Tomi is too old now to believe this fairy tale. But every time just before he plucks a carrot from Emma-mama's garden, for a minute, just for a minute of a minute, he thinks… maybe.

It usually takes a couple of tugs to pull them up. After the first tough tug, they slip out as smoothly as a Hajdú's sword from its sheath. Each time he and Gabi pull one out, they race to the well, haul up a bucketful of water, dunk the carrots into the sharp cold water and with their fingernails scrape off the earth till the carrot's orange skin glistens. And every time, before he takes that first crunchy bite, he closes his eyes like his father taught him, to give thanks for the juicy sweetness that is about to fill his mouth, and smiles.

—

Tomi's Golden Green is on the other side of the picket fence. He has never been to the real Golden Green. He has only seen the pitch in the photos of *The People's Sport News* and through his father's description, "a beautiful soft green carpet, so green and so soft that you want to sleep on it." Every time his father goes to Budapest, Tomi begs his father to take him.

"It's too far and you're too young," his mother always tells him. But the last time his father was getting ready to leave, he promised Tomi that on his eighth birthday, two long, long months away, he would take him. Until then, he can only imagine the Golden Green. And he does. He closes his eyes and he is there. For ninety wonderful minutes on those Sunday afternoons when the Honvéd, his favourite soccer team, plays, he, his father and Gabi sit glued to the radio listening to the broadcast of the game.

It was the play-by-play commentator who nicknamed the People's Stadium pitch the "Golden Green." According to him, it is the most beautiful soccer pitch in the world. He says so every Sunday as he introduces the line-ups and announces the attendance. His words paint such exciting pictures it's almost as if Tomi's at the game. His description of the action makes Tomi's jaw clench and heart beat fast. Sitting still is impossible. Though it is hard for him to imagine a stadium that can hold 65,000 people, he has no trouble hearing the sound of 65,000 fans: their 65,000 "ooohhhs" after a missed chance, their 65,000 "ahhhs" after each fantastic save by Grosics, and the deafening roar of 65,000 cheering fans whenever the Honvéd score. He, his father and Gabi always join in, even more loudly when the goal scorer is Puskás.

—

Immediately after each of those Sunday games, his friends come over and they replay the match. The pebbly dirt yard, with the chicken coop at one end and the outhouse at the other, is transformed into the Golden Green. Overturned chicken-feed buckets become goalposts; the fences on the well and outhouse sides become touchlines.

They stand at attention and sing the national anthem.

O, my God, the Magyar bless
With Thy plenty and good cheer
With Thine aid his just cause press,
Where his foes to fight appear.
Fate, who for so long did'st frown

Bring him happy times and ways;
Atoning sorrow hath weighed down
Sins of past and future days.

They line up for the pretend team photo. After Carrot says "click," the two captains, Frog and Gabi, shake hands and exchange their homemade team flags just as they see it done in photos of *The People's Sport News*. And before they begin, they, like the linesmen who make sure that the nets have no holes in them, make sure that all chickens are in the coop and that the outhouse door is tightly shut.

During the match, they take on their heroes' names, they become their heroes. And whenever he, "Tomi Puskás," scores, he has no trouble hearing the 65,000 fans cheering him.

But now that he is almost eight, and has grown almost a head taller than the picket fence, the field feels small. There is less space for his weaving dribbles, less room to execute the head-and-run. His kick is stronger and when the ball strikes the hen house, the thud sends the chickens into a clucking frenzy. They fly about the coop and became too nervous to lay eggs. And when the ball is booted into the rose bushes, petals fly everywhere, causing Emma-mama to come running after them, shouting and swinging her broom, usually ending the game.

Tomi hears Red crow, closes his eyes and imagines that 65,000 fans are calling his name.

—

"Tomi! Tomi! Where are you?"

It isn't his mother's normal voice, the one she uses when she wants him to come in for supper or run an errand. This one sounds different. It's one he started to hear only recently.

"I'm here, Mama."

He hears her let out a deep sigh as soon as she sees him and sees the worry on her face disappear. "Ah. My little rooster is out on his perch. Did you wake Red? Why are you up so early?"

"I'm going to school today."

"Ah, yes. It's exciting, isn't it? You're a big boy now. And it looks like it's going to be a beautiful first day. Go get dressed while I make breakfast."

"Can I have breakfast with the blacksmiths?"

Her face gets serious, the way it usually does when she is about to say no to something he wants to do.

"All right, but first get dressed."

"Be careful not to get your clothes dirty," Emma-mama shouts as Tomi and Gabi hurry to the blacksmiths', each cradling a mug of milk and a thick slice of rye bread.

The blacksmiths' yard next door is twice the size of his Golden Green and is always filled with wagons with broken axles, buggies with cracked shafts and wheels with missing spokes. He imagines them as injured creatures brought to the blacksmiths to be healed. And the blacksmiths, like doctors and sorcerers, make them strong and healthy again.

"Attila, stay!" Gabi shouts as the huge German shepherd comes charging at them. Attila does it every time they come over. Tomi is used to his charge. He likes the way Attila rises on his hind legs and plops his two thick, leathery front paws on his chest, almost knocking him over. His breath is hot and he always tries to lick Tomi's face with his slobbering tongue. Tomi likes the friendly fight to get him off. But today he doesn't want his dirty paws on his clean clothes.

"Stay!" He shouts and holds his cup and slice of bread away from his clothes. Attila comes to an immediate halt, turns, and wagging his tail, trots ahead of them back to the hearth where he plunks himself down and with tongue half out, pants and waits.

The smithy is at the far end of the yard, a large wooden building with a barn-sized door that's always open, warm and welcoming. Every time he steps inside, Tomi feels like he is in a world of giants from a long time ago. Two of the three walls are covered with ox yokes to be braced, horse collars to be tacked, scythes and sickles to be sharpened, broken wheels to be mended, barrel hoops to be rejoined and stacks of silvery horseshoes waiting to be fitted on mighty steeds. And hung neatly on the third wall are the blacksmiths' tools: sharp chisels, pointy punches, wrenches and clamps with wide mouths and heavy hammers and scary tongs of all sizes. And, rising in the middle of the barn from the huge blackened brick hearth is a big chimney right up through the roof. It's the only chimney in Békes the storks never build a nest on because smoke comes out of it all year round. On one side of the hearth are logs and kindling neatly stacked as high as Tomi. On its other side is a large bin filled to the brim with shiny black lumps of coal.

It's Fire's job to rekindle the hearth every morning and keep it going all day. All day long he splits logs, chops kindling, shovels coal, hauls iron bars and carries buckets of water. It's hard work but Fire is strong. He has big arms and shoulders and he never complains. He's always smiling and whistling.

Tomi remembers when Fire, whose real name is Imi, first came to work at the smithy last spring and was trying to start a fire in the hearth. Zoli, whom Tomi calls Dragon Mouth and who was responsible for teaching Fire, told him that he had to stack the kindling in an upside-down pyramid shape because it was the best way to get the fire started. Fire tried and tried but couldn't.

"You'll never be a blacksmith if you can't do that!" Dragon Mouth yelled each time he failed.

After a number of tries, Jóska, the chief blacksmith, slapped Imi upside the head. "You fool. Can't you figure it out? Zoli's pulling your leg."

Imi smiled sheepishly, and walked away, rubbing his head. Later, when he got the fire real hot, he reached in and grabbed a glowing piece of coal.

"Zoli! Catch!" he shouted and lobbed the red-hot coal toward him.

"Fire!" Zoli yelled as he caught it and juggled it from one hand to the other and flipped it back to Imi, who turned and lobbed it to Jóska, who caught it, also juggled it like a hot potato and threw it back to Imi. They did this, shouting and laughing all the time, until the coal cooled and Imi dropped it back into the hearth. From that moment on, everybody called Imi Fire.

Zoli, besides being the joker, is in charge of the Dragon. That's what Tomi calls the bellows. The large heart-shaped wood panels joined together with strips of leather are suspended from a crossbeam, and by squeezing the wooden panels together, like an accordion, Zoli forces the air in the leather pouch to whoosh out the nozzle into the hearth like a loud breath. And from the hearth flames rise. Tomi loves watching the bursts of flames rush out and shoot skywards. Zoli makes the coals glow so red and so hot that when Jóska places an iron bar into the hearth, almost instantly it begins to transform from a hard metal into a white-red shimmering transparent glow.

Jóska is a fiery giant. Wearing his black leather apron, with his large tongs he lifts the white-hot bars of iron out of the hearth as though he were picking up toothpicks. And when he places one on his anvil and begins pounding, sparks, like shooting stars, fly everywhere. Once Jóska starts hammering, the clanging is almost as loud as the church bell and can be heard streets away. When he does this, Tomi often has to cover his ears. Jóska is that giant sorcerer who can make anything out of fire and iron. He shapes the iron bars into those horseshoes, barrel hoops, scythes, sickles and sometimes even swords that decorate the walls. If he weren't going to be the next Puskás, Tomi would want to be a blacksmith like Joska.

———

Tomi and Gabi like Jóska, Zoli and Fire because they are always joking, laughing, shouting, singing or whistling while they work; and they always let them play in the yard. And like today, they often wave them over for breakfast.

"Good morning, boys," shout the blacksmiths in unison as they thread slabs of back bacon, onions, and green peppers onto their skewers.

The boys pour their milk into a small enamel pot that Jóska hangs above the glowing embers. Tomi watches the teardrops of fat form on the edges of the slabs of bacon. He enjoys listening to the hissing bacon, watching the tiny puffs of steam rise and the tears drop one by one on the slices that Zoli slides under the skewers.

Rabbi Stern, in one of his lessons, told the boys that Jews aren't allowed to eat pork because pigs are dirty animals and they don't chew their cud. Tomi doesn't know what "cud" means because the rabbi didn't explain, but he knows from being around chickens, ducks, geese and pigs that they are always pecking at or sitting or rolling in dirt. He doesn't see how animals cannot be dirty. Also Gabi's father sometimes brings home slabs of ham. And ham, he knows is a part of a pig. And his parents know that the blacksmiths smear their bread with bacon fat but have never told the boys that they weren't allowed to eat it. How can it be wrong if it smells so good and if it's so tasty? The sizzling bacon always makes his mouth water.

The boys sit on small iron stools with legs like dragon's feet and backrests in the shape of dragon wings that Jóska and Zoli forged for them. Whenever he sits there, Tomi feels like one of the fabulous Gypsy Kings in Frog's mother's stories.

"Sit," Gabi orders Attila, who is nosing in for a bite. Tomi tears off a piece of his bread and flings it into the air. Attila leaps up, twists his body, snaps the bread in mid-air and gulps it down in one swallow before sitting back down again, contentedly licking his lips.

Tomi leans forward as he takes careful sips and bites. He doesn't want stains on his brand new freshly ironed white shirt or on his polished shoes, which he only recently learned to tie.

"Why so fancy today?" Zoli asks.

"I'm going to school."

"No!" the blacksmiths cry out in unison.

"So you won't be helping us anymore?" Zoli says, looking sad.

"Oh, yes, I will."

He can't imagine not being around Attila and the blacksmiths, not hearing the clanging of hammers, not watching the dragon flames or the clouds of hissing steam when Jóska dips glowing iron into a cold bucket of water. He can't imagine not stroking the horses' muzzles while they are being shod, not stacking kindling, and not throwing lumps of coal into the mouth of the dragon. And the blacksmiths had promised they would make swords for the boys.

"Gabi! Tomi! It's time."

2

Sanyi caught the earliest express train to Budapest. As the train sped through the early dawn, he reread the letter for the third time.

April 1, 1949

Kistarcsa Rehabilitation Labour Camp
County of Pest
Ministry of Home Affairs

Notice of Appearance
By order of The Office of the Secretary for State Security
People's Republic of Hungary

Sándor Wolfstein

You are hereby officially notified that Dezsö Földember and Emma Földember have been arrested by the Hungarian State Security Police for crimes against the People's Republic of Hungary. You are listed as the next of kin. Their child, Gábor Földember, is in the People's Security Nursery at Kistarcsa. If you wish to accept the responsibility of guardianship, you are to appear at the Nursery on Monday, April 4, 1949 at 14h30. Failure to comply will make Gábor Földember a ward of the state.

By noon Sanyi was standing outside the Western Train Station in Budapest, wondering how to get to the prison. He knew it was on the outskirts of the city but he didn't know how to get there. He asked a couple of passersby, but they only shook their heads and hurried on their way.

"Comrade. Come over here!"

He turned to see two police officers standing at the corner of the street. The shorter one was waving him over. Sanyi stiffened.

"I said come over here. Are you deaf?"

He took a deep breath and walked towards them.

"Where are you from? Show us your Identity Book."

"Comrade Officers, I am from Hajdubékes," he said as calmly as he could. "Would you be kind enough to tell me how to get to Kistarcsa?"

"Why are you in Budapest?" the short one asked, as his partner looked over the document. "Why do you want to go to Kistarcsa?"

Sanyi handed him the letter. The officer read it slowly. He passed it to his partner and eyed Sanyi suspiciously. Sanyi knew better than to make eye contact. He looked down and stared at their immaculately polished shoes. They returned his papers and gave him directions to the bus terminal at the back of the train station.

"Thank you, Comrade Officers," Sanyi said, and hurried off.

Kistarcsa, the town, was fifteen kilometres east of Budapest. The Rehabilitation Labour Camp was located outside the town. The forbidding grey structure, with guard towers at each corner and walls topped with barbed wire, stood in the middle of a bare grey field. Nothing else existed for acres. No other buildings, no trees and no vegetation.

The overcast sky made the place seem even bleaker than it was. He remembered when he had been a prisoner himself, he had preferred grey days; he always felt worse when the sun was out. Under grey skies, guards, prisoners and even those leading normal lives on the outside, were under a similar gloom. But under a sunny blue sky, a prisoner is keenly reminded of his imprisonment, his loss of freedom. He is not permitted to stop and savour the sunny day; he is denied the simple joy of standing still, closing his eyes and feeling the glow, the warmth on his face and nothing else. And no one telling him he couldn't. No one yelling at him *"Schnell! Move!"*

Sanyi arrived thirty minutes before he was due. A guard took the letter and his Identity Book and told him to wait. He was used to waiting in such places. Waiting had been a way of life when he was a prisoner: waiting in line to be counted before going to work, waiting before eating, waiting before going to the bathroom, waiting before coming back from work, and waiting before going to sleep. He remembered waiting for no other reason than that the guards felt like making you wait.

So, he waited. He had heard horror stories about the Kistarcsa Prison. Before the war it was a transfer point of thousands of Jews to Auschwitz. Now, under Communism, it was a rehabilitation labour camp.

The guard returned and ordered Sanyi to follow him into a large empty room. The small windows at the far end were too high for any view of the outside. The light that shone in looked starved, afraid and grey. At the centre of the floor, under a row of bare light bulbs, ran two red parallel lines about a metre apart.

The guard pointed at the line on the right. "Stand here," he commanded.

A few minutes later, Emma was brought in. She was wearing a grey prison smock with a number on it. Her hair was uncombed, and her face looked haggard, as if she hadn't slept in weeks. Her eyes were puffy and red from crying.

"My baby! Sanyi, they took Gabi! Where is my baby?"

"Be quiet!" the guard snapped. "Do not speak until you are given permission. Stand here." He pointed to the line parallel to Sanyi's.

"They won't let me see him!"

The guard grabbed Emma's arm roughly. "Didn't you hear me? No talking!"

Sanyi put his fingers to his lips and mouthed, "Shhhhh."

Emma gulped a few deep breaths. Her sobs subsided to sniffles.

"You can talk now, but no whispering and no touching. Understood?"

"Yes, sir," they replied in unison, like schoolchildren.

"Gabi is okay," Sanyi reassured her. "He's in the nursery. He's okay. I'm going to take him home with me. We'll take care of him and we'll come and visit."

"I want to see him. I want my baby!" Emma's sobs began to overwhelm her again. She reached out and fell into Sanyi's arms.

The guard standing beside her slapped the back of Emma's head. "I said no touching!" Sanyi stood motionless, feeling an old familiar helplessness as they dragged her away.

Sanyi was led out of the room along a windowless corridor. "Comrade, may I see her husband, Dezső Földember?"

"No. He's in solitary confinement."

Halfway along the corridor, Sanyi stopped. "Comrade, may I tie my shoelaces?"

The guard looked down at Sanyi's shoes and nodded. He knelt and fiddled with his laces.

"Pardon me, Comrade Officer, you dropped this," he said as he stood up and handed an envelope to the guard. The guard looked around. Wordlessly, he took it and slid it in his pocket.

Sanyi followed the guard down the stairs. It was even greyer and damper than outside. A row of steel doors ran along either side of the stinking corridor. He opened one. Sanyi hesitated. It was dark. He couldn't see a thing. What if the guard locked the door once he stepped inside? Who would know? What could he do?

"Dezső? Are you there?"

"Sanyi?"

Reluctantly, he stepped inside. As his eyes adjusted to the dark, he made out an outline hunched on the floor against the wall. "Yes. It's me. Are you all right?"

"I'm okay."

"What happened?" Sanyi asked, kneeling close to Dezsö.

"Have you seen Emma? Gabi?"

"They're both okay. What happened?"

Dezsö grunted. "We got to Sopron, where we met the man I hired to guide us across No Man's Land. Damn him. He was a police informant. The border guards were waiting for us...What's going to happen to Gabi?"

"I'm taking him home with me. We'll bring him for visits."

"Good. Thanks. What a damned country. These Communist crazies took away my land, the land my family owned and worked for generations. They declare that it belongs to all the people. So everyone owns it. And if you object, they say, 'Too bad, Comrade.' They say, 'If you don't like it, leave.' And when you say 'O.K. I want to leave,' they say you can't." Dezsö spat.

"Enough of that!" the guard yelled. "Now, you, out!"

"We'll come and visit," Sanyi promised before the door clanged shut.

He was led into another windowless room, where a woman in a military uniform sitting at a desk took his Identity Book and ordered him to go sit on the bench in the corridor. He sat and waited while she slowly examined each page, then put the book to the side, pulled out some forms from her desk drawer and shuffled and reordered them. The guard stood at attention outside the door.

"Sándor Wolfstein," she called out.

The guard escorted him in. Sanyi looked past her into the nursery. He counted six small beds and six cribs. Each had a number on the footboard.

"Are you related to the prisoners?"

"Yes."

"To which?"

"The wife, Emma Földember."

"How are you related?"

"Cousins."

"Do you accept their guilt?"

Sanyi hesitated.

The woman looked up.

"Yes."

"Do accept their punishment as just?"

"Yes."

"Do you accept responsibility for the child?"

"Yes."

"Why?"

He said nothing. The woman looked up again.

"Family," he said. The word felt strange to him. How bare the family tree had become. Mothers, fathers, aunts, uncles, brothers, sisters, and cousins had been lopped off, gone. Almost everyone killed. Emma and Dezsö's son Gabi had been the first new branch and just last year Hannah and Sanyi's son Tomi. He wondered "why start again?" But they did.

"Family," he repeated to himself.

When the matron finished questioning him she waved him back to the bench. Then she looked down again and scribbled some notes on the file. Sanyi watched her, the way a cat watches a mouse, casually but intently. She was a plump matronly woman with greying hair pulled into a bun. Whenever she needed to think, she gnawed on the tip of the pencil. She often licked the lead before pressing down hard on the paper. She wrote slowly, as if the task was painful. When she finally finished, she lit a cigarette, inhaled deeply and held it, savouring it for as long as possible before slowly blowing the smoke through her nostrils. He watched and waited. She stubbed out the cigarette and carefully stored the butt in the little tin box on her desk. She rose from her chair and plodded over to one of the cribs, where she picked up a child and brought it to him.

"Comrade. How do I know it's the right boy?" Sanyi asked as he held the child at arm's length.

"It's written here in the files. Child 6, Gábor Földember."

"Comrade, I really can't tell one baby from another."

The matron tapped the file impatiently with her nicotine-stained finger. "Do you question a government document?"

"No, by no means, but…"

"No buts," she snapped and went to fetch the baby's clothes. While she was gone, Sanyi pulled back the diaper and saw that it was a boy and that he was circumcised. He readjusted the diaper and took a pack of cigarettes from his pocket. He placed it on the woman's desk.

When she returned, she eyed the pack and then Sanyi.

"Here are his clothes," she said, her voice softening.

"Comrade, please, let me show him to his mother so I can be certain. My wife will kill me if I show up with the wrong baby. You know men and babies." He smiled.

She quickly slipped the pack of cigarettes into her pocket. "All right." She sighed. "Take him back to the visitors' room," the matron ordered the guard. Again Sanyi waited.

When Emma saw Gabi, she broke free from her guard and ran for him. "My baby, my baby!" she cried, kissing him all over. The guard grabbed her by the hair and tried to pull her back, but Emma was too strong for her. She held onto Sanyi's arm with all her strength. A second guard ran over to pry her hands loose.

"My baby. My baby!" she cried as they dragged her away wailing, writhing, wriggling and twisting to take a last look. "Gabi! Gabi!"

Sanyi winked as he took Gabi's hand and waved it.

All the way home, Gabi cried. He threw up and got diarrhoea. Sanyi spent the entire train ride trying to calm him down and clean him up. By the time they got to Békés, he and Gabi were a filthy, smelly mess. When Hannah saw the two of them, she didn't know whether to laugh or cry. So she did both.

And so it was that Tomi suddenly had a big brother and Hannah and Sándor Wolfstein were parents of two.

As she bathed and changed Gabi, Hannah found herself marvelling once again that she was a mother. After the war, Hannah had returned home full of anger and shame. She knew she didn't deserve to live. If not for Magda, she probably never would have survived. But then she had met up with Sanyi again, who had returned to Békes as broken as she. And they had wed, the marriage of two ghosts. When she discovered she was with child, Hannah's anger turned to fear. She couldn't imagine being a mother. How could she possibly protect a child when she had done nothing to save her mother and little sister?

But now, as she washes Gabi clean, she feels dangerous.

—

When Emma and Dezsö returned to Békes two years later, they no longer had a place to live. As part of their punishment, their home had been given to another family. Sanyi and Hannah divided their two-bedroom house in half. Gabi was reunited with his parents but he had a hard time calling them Mama and Papa, even though Sanyi and Hannah had taken him to visit them every month. For a long while, Gabi, like Tomi, called them Emma-mama and Dezsö-papa.

3

"We're going with you."

"Why? I can go by myself! And anyway, I'm going with Gabi."

"We want to go with you on your first day. It's a special day for us too. Now go and get your schoolbag."

He knows it's useless to argue with his mother once she's made up her mind. And secretly, he doesn't mind. He is a little scared. He goes to get his schoolbag, making sure that his ruler, pencil case and two notebooks are inside. Last night, he and his mother—actually his mother did it while he watched—carefully wrapped each notebook in butcher's wax paper and glued subject tags on the front. His mother used her beautiful handwriting to label them "Arithmetic," "Composition," as well as his name—Tamás Wolfstein. She is proud of her penmanship and has tried to teach him to write like her before he began school. He tried but he couldn't work the nib without smudging the pages.

While his mother wrote, his father checked the nibs of his pen and made sure the cap of the ink bottle was on tight.

"Now we have to sharpen your pencil," his father said, and reached into his pocket to take out his pocketknife. He extended his closed hand towards Tomi, and when he opened it, Tomi saw in his palm two knives, his father's and a similar but smaller one.

"Now that you are going to school, you will need this," his father said, handing him the smaller one.

"Oh, Papa, it's beautiful." He hugged his father.

"Yours even has a spring." His father pressed a button and the blade jumped out.

The knife had a knobby elkhorn handle and a sharp curved blade. When Tomi slid his thumb along the cool metallic edge of the blade, he felt grown up.

"You be careful with that," his mother said. "It's not a toy. Don't you cut yourself with it."

"Now, I'll show you how to sharpen your pencil," his father said.

Tomi held the knife in his palm as if it were a delicate baby sparrow. He closed his fingers around the knobby handle, feeling its gnarls. He brandished it as he might a sword. His mother looked up from writing and gave him a stern look.

"I told you, it's not a toy."

"I know."

He spent the rest of the evening, until bedtime, practising on pieces of kindling, imitating his father. He held the kindling in his left while his right held the knife, thumb pushing the back of the blade.

"Not so deep," his father told him. "Like this, like a soft pass and a follow through, the way Puskás does it." Soon, his blade was sliding smoothly. The shavings curled and dropped as he brought the tips of the kindling to a fine point. He was ready for school.

—

Tomi lives on Hajdú Street, not far from The People's Elementary School. Nothing is very far away in Békes. In many ways, it is still a village, with cows and geese trudging along dirt roads and sidewalks on their way to pasture. Most families have vegetable gardens and keep chickens and pigs, that they slaughter themselves. They bake their own bread in outdoor kilns and draw water from the corner pumps. There are still homes without electricity and running water. And most, like his, have outhouses.

As they walk toward the school, his parents nod to the people they meet along the way.

"In Békes everybody knows everybody," his father has said many times.

"And everybody knows everybody's business, even if it's none of their business," his mother replied every time.

Békes, like most towns, had grown around the old market square. It used to be a very busy place, where once a week the local farmers brought their produce, tradesmen their pots and pans to sell, and Gypsies their horses, jewellery and fortune-telling skills. It was where news, gossip and rumour was heard, started and spread. It still is, but after the war, under Communism, everything had been nationalized and only those with small gardens, like the villagers, are allowed to sell. The market has shrunk and has become more of a gathering place, where on summer Sundays after a soccer game or supper, old men in their Sunday suits, collarless shirts and black fedoras sit on park benches, lean on their canes, smoke their pipes, stare into the distance, and talk, occasionally, about how much better it was in the old days, while their wives in black dresses, shawls and head scarves watch young children run about, "tsk-tsk" about the children's lack of respect and scrutinize and pass judgement on the young men strolling back and forth across the square in front of chaperoned young girls.

In the centre of the square, on a large granite pedestal, stands a statue of a Russian soldier cradling a machine gun. His head held high, the soldier stares into the distance. "Before the war it used to be a Hajdú, with his sword drawn, like this." His father posed.

Tomi imagines the Hajdús to be like the Hussars in the book his parents gave him for his last birthday, dashing warriors wielding beautiful scimitar-curved swords, riding fiery stallions and charging into battle against the Turks.

"Did you know that a long, long, long…"

"…time ago…"

"…the Hajdús lived in this county. That's why the county is called Hajdú," his father told him when he gave him the book, "because a long, long, long…"

"…time ago…"

"…they were given land here as a reward for their bravery against the Turks and the Hapsburgs. And towns like Békes, Dobos and Szabad honoured them with statues."

"So why do we have a Russian soldier now?"

"Because the Russian soldiers liberated us from the bad Hungarians and Germans. A lot of them died, so the town erected a statue to honour them."

"Because the cowardly city council was told by the Ruskies to tear down the Hajdú statue and put up this one," Gabi's father interjected. "And they, like frightened sheep, obeyed. But what they don't teach you is that the Hajdús were thieves and bullies. It's always thieves and bullies that get statues erected in their honour."

Gabi's father is always saying things like that. He seems to have something bad to say about everything and everyone. Tomi doesn't care. What Tomi most wants to be, after being like Puskás, and a blacksmith, is a Hajdú.

Behind the statue is the City Hall. Built to replace the previous bombed-out one, the three-storey, grey stucco building with large black curtained windows is the highest and biggest building in town. To the right of the statue is the church with its single tall bell tower.

Tomi had been up there once with his father when his father was doing fire-watch duty.

"What town is over there?" his father asked, pointing out the south window of the tower.

"Dobos," he answered proudly.

"Very good. And what's there?" his father asked, pointing out the north window.

"The cemetery."

"Right again. That's where my father, your grandfather who never saw you, may he rest in peace, lies."

"And Grandma?"

"She's not there."

"Where is she?"

"And there?" his father's finger pointed out the east window.

"That's The People's Collective Farm."

"See how big it is? It used to belong to Dezsö-papa's family. They had a lot of land and were very rich."

"How come they don't have it now?"

"Because now it is shared with everybody. And what is over that way?" he asked, pointing through the western window.

"The Békes Golden Green!" he shouted.

The shimmery manicured green that was Békes's soccer field was just past the railroad tracks. Gabi, Tomi and Tomi's father, the scout for the team, spent many of their spring and fall evenings watching the team practise. During breaks, the players let Tomi and Gabi play. Gabi practised his panther-leap saves at one end, while at the other end, Tomi worked on his dribbling and shooting skills. And in vain, of course, the players tried to take the ball away from him, stop him from dribbling the ball between their legs. He always beat the last defender with his right-to-left foot shift and broke in alone on the goalie, faking him with a head deke. And as the goalie dove one way, Tomi would shoot the ball into the opposite top corner. It worked every time.

The school is adjacent to the church. It's a rectangular one-storey, pale-blue stucco building with big windows. Because Gabi started school last year, Tomi, a year younger, often went to meet him at the end of classes. He liked to arrive early, stand beneath the window of Gabi's class and listen to the students reciting in unison the ABCs, a poem or some other lesson. His mother knew Gabi's teacher, and so occasionally he was allowed to attend, even though he wasn't yet a student. On those special days, he sat quietly next to Gabi and listened to Mrs. Gombás tell tales of the Hajdús and their glorious battles and remind the students that everybody should be proud of them.

"Here we are." His mother kneels to adjust his shirt. She hugs him tightly. He squirms. He doesn't want to be seen being hugged and kissed by his mother. Now that he's in grade one, he isn't a baby anymore. Gabi steps back out of hugging range and waits for Tomi.

"Have a good day." Solemnly, Tomi's father shakes hands with the boys.

—

Hannah and Sanyi watch the boys walk through the wrought-iron gate into the schoolyard. "Hard to believe that Tomi is already in school."

"Time passes so quickly."

"There was a time when I thought time had stopped."

"I remember a time when I couldn't even imagine such a day."

"There were days when I didn't care if I lived or died."

"But we live." Sanyi moves closer to her. "And I'm glad."

"Sanyi, I see signs of bad times again. I'm scared."

"But at least in school they're safe."

"I hope so." Hannah leans into Sanyi.

Mrs. Gombás stands in the yard, assembling the students by twos according to size. Tomi, one of the smaller ones, stands near the front. Gabi, in Small Potato's class, is in the line next to his.

"Small Potato is the worst," Gabi told him last night.

"His name is Mr. Toth," his mother corrected him. "You have to respect your teacher."

"Why is he called Small Potato?"

"Because he's small and has bug eyes like a potato. He has a big ruler and he uses it a lot. If you're caught not sitting up straight or not paying attention—whack! If you answer a question without standing up beside your desk with your hands by your side—whack! He makes you come to the front, hold out your palm, and—whack!"

Tomi listened, transfixed.

"And if you're caught talking in class, you have to hold out your hand with the fingertips pressed together like this." Gabi took Tomi's fingers and huddled them. They looked like frightened children. "And then…" Gabi raised his ruler in mid-air, paused.

Tomi was wide-eyed.

"Whack!" Gabi shouted as he brought down the ruler. Tomi yanked his hand away. "If you move your hand, you get it twice." Gabi laughed.

Mrs. Gombás claps her hands. "All right now. Let's march smartly into class." To her rhythmic clapping, Tomi marches happily toward his new adventure.

———

It's the same classroom Gabi was in last year, the one he sat in, mesmerized by stories of the Hajdús. It's a large room with a high ceiling and three large windows. The students are seated alphabetically in six rows of polished double desks lined up exactly behind one another. Tomi's is the last desk in the last row. Frog is his desk mate. Tomi is surprised to see Frog sitting next to him because he knows that the letter F comes way before W. He's about to ask Frog why he's been put there but then remembers Gabi's warning about talking in class. He doesn't want to get whacked with the ruler on the first day. He turns, reaches into his schoolbag, takes out his ink bottle and carefully positions it in the inkwell. He lays the pencil case next to it and tucks his notebooks into the shelf under the desk. When he finishes he places his intertwined fingers on his desk. "My desk," he thinks.

Frog takes out a crumpled piece of paper from his pants' pocket, smooths it with his palm and takes a stub of a pencil from his shirt pocket, which he lays on the crumpled paper. Then he entwines his fingers like Tomi and smiles.

A crackling sound comes from the loudspeaker above the door. "Stand!" Mrs. Gombás commands the class. "We will begin every morning by listening to the national anthem," she says, pointing to the loudspeaker. "And when we listen to the national anthem, we stand at attention beside our desk and we look at Comrade Marx, Comrade Lenin, Comrade Stalin and Comrade Rákosi." She points to the pictures of each on the wall above the blackboard. "Does everyone understand?"

"Yes, Mrs. Gombás," they reply in unison.

"Now sit," she says after the anthem. "In school you will learn many things, but the first thing you will learn is how to be a good Hungarian and a good Communist. And the first rule of being a good Hungarian is to be proud. Hungary is a great country filled with brave people and a proud history. You will learn about these people and their deeds."

Grosics, Lantos, Buzansky, Lorant, Zakarias, Bozsik, Cibor, Hidegkuti, Budai, Kocsis and Puskás, 6-3 and 7-1. Tomi recites to himself the Hungarian National team players' names and the scores they beat England by.

"A good Hungarian respects his parents and his country. A good Hungarian is always on guard against its enemies. And to be a good Communist you must follow the rules. Rules give us order and order gives us peace and prosperity. Following rules makes us collectively strong. Does everyone understand?"

"Yes, Mrs. Gombás," they reply again as one.

"Good. Now here are the rules of the class that you must obey. First. When you are sitting, you must have your hands on your desk like this," she says, extending her own hands, her fingers interlaced. "Second. When you answer a question, you must raise your right hand with your index and middle finger pointing to the ceiling, like this. Third. When I call upon you to answer, you must stand up straight beside your desk, without fidgeting, and respond clearly. Does everybody understand?"

"Yes, Mrs. Gombás."

"Good. Now we will begin with the alphabet. We will recite it together."

With her pointer Mrs. Gombás taps each of the letters painted above the blackboard. She moves the pointer, keeping the rhythm and directing the class to sound like one voice. She makes the class repeat it half a dozen times.

"Béla Vándor. Come to the front!"

To Tomi's surprise Frog stands. This is the first time he has ever heard Frog called Béla. Frog is his best friend, the one he and Gabi usually play soccer with. In a way, the boys have known each other before they knew each other. Frog's mother, who washes clothes for his family, always brought Frog along with her, so the boys learned to crawl, walk and play soccer together. She once told Tomi that he was her child too because she gave him milk when he was a baby because his mother couldn't. She said that she even gave Gabi milk. He didn't understand how giving him milk made Frog's mother his mother. When he told his mother she got angry and told him not to believe crazy Gypsy talk. She was his only mother.

Everyone calls him Frog, even his own mother. Frog loves frogs. When they aren't playing soccer, the boys spend their time catching frogs in the marsh next to Frog's house. Frog is much better at it than Tomi or Gabi. He sits on his haunches, as still as the frog he's trying to catch, and quietly leans over the lily pad or rock it's perched atop to whisper:

Frog, frog, little frog, leap into my little hand
Frog, frog, little frog, eat up what makes me sad.
Frog, frog, little frog, in my aching belly
Devour the devil to make me strong and healthy.

Then, with one hand, he slaps the water to startle the frog into leaping while his other, quick as a frog's tongue, darts out to catch it in mid-air. Most of the frogs they catch they give to Frog's mother, who uses them to make potions and remedies. But Frog always keeps one as a pet. It's not unusual to hear burps coming from one of Frog's pockets.

The boys are inseparable. So when it came time for Tomi to start school, Frog announced that he wanted to go too. This surprised Frog's mother and she told him not to be a fool, but Tomi's mother encouraged her to let him go. She even gave Frog's mother an almost-new shirt and a pair of pants with only a couple of patches. So Frog became the first Gypsy kid in town to attend school.

Frog shuffles to the front.

"Walk properly, not like a Gypsy," Mrs. Gombás snaps. She places her hand on his head and firmly turns him to face the class.

"Now, recite."

Frog gets the first few letters right but gets confused after G. Tomi jerks when Mrs. Gombás smacks Frog across the back of his head. Several slaps later, Frog is done and back at his desk, sniffling quietly. Mrs. Gombás pulls a handkerchief from her pocket and wipes her hands.

"Tamás Wolfstein, come to the front."

He's afraid. He walks slowly, haltingly, lifting his feet higher than usual. He looks at Mrs. Gombás. She has her hand to her mouth. He doesn't know if she is angry or not. When he finally gets to the front, she takes him by the shoulders and gently turns him to face the class.

"Recite!"

He swivels his head to see if she's angry. She places her palm firmly on his head and turns it back to face the class.

"Recite!"

He begins slowly, making a great effort to pronounce each letter properly and clearly. Even though he's practised with his mother and Gabi, he pauses after each letter, expecting a slap.

When he finishes, he closes his eyes and waits.

"*This* is how it's done," she says, patting him on the head. On his way back to his seat, he turns and sees a smile on her face.

He loves being in school.

—

"Rotten ABC. Rotten Mrs. Gombás," Frog grumbles as they head out the door to meet Gabi. "I hate her."

"Yeah," says Tomi, but with little enthusiasm.

Carrot and Gabi are waiting for them in the yard. "We're gonna play here after lunch. Are you guys coming?" Carrot asks.

"Sure."

"Tomi! Gabi!"

Tomi wasn't expecting his mother, but there she is waiting for him at the gate. He isn't happy to see her. He and Gabi were going to go to the Kiosk before heading home.

"Why can't I?" he asks.

"I'll tell you later," she says firmly.

"Good-bye, Mrs. Wolfstein. We'll see you guys later." Carrot says.

"Small Potato already whacked Szeles!" Gabi tells Tomi.

"And Mrs. Gombás slapped Frog," Tomi adds.

"They probably deserved it," says his mother as she takes them both by the hand.

Tomi knows it's useless to complain about teachers to his parents. Teachers are always right. His parents always talked about how wise teachers were, and how important learning was and how they wished they themselves could have had more schooling.

As they set off across the town square he sees a crowd has gathered in front of the statue of the Russian soldier. He feels his mother's hand tighten around his. A man stands at the base of the statue and is shouting and waving his hand.

"Why is that man shouting?"

"He isn't shouting. He's reciting a poem," Gabi says.

"How do you know?"

"Because we learned that poem last year. You'll probably learn it too."

"What poem?"

"Arise, Hungarians," his mother answers and picks up her pace. "Now let's hurry!"

"Can we stay and listen to him?" Tomi pleads. He likes crowds. They are so exciting with people cheering and yelling. You get to feel strong. Just like at soccer games. He knows his mother likes poetry. Often, he drifts off to sleep listening to his mother's sing-song voice reciting a poem she herself learned in school.

"No."

"Why not?"

"Because it's not for us," she says. "Now hurry up!"

—

Tomi smells it from the verandah.

"The aroma of slowly cooked paprika-spiced chicken is like a warm hug," Emma-mama says.

"You say that about all food, Mama," Gabi says.

"That's because it's true, my dear son." She hugs Gabi and gives him a loud kiss on top of his head.

Gabi's mother sways to the music as she stirs the pot, humming as she usually does while she cooks and cleans. One time Tomi saw her on the verandah dancing with the broom.

"I was going to be a dancer," she often tells the boys. When Gabi once asked her why she didn't become one, she answered, "People don't dance during war. And then we were taken away."

"Who took you away? Where?" Tomi asked. She just fell silent and began to cry. The boys never asked again.

Tomi likes Emma-mama because most times she is happy, not like his mother, who is serious most of the time. Emma-mama likes to laugh, especially at Tomi's father's jokes. Tomi doesn't understand most of them, but he enjoys watching Emma-mama explode with laughter. It starts with a short snort, and then she takes a deep breath and stops. Then her belly starts to jiggle. His father takes this as his cue to tell her another. Soon, eyes watering, she's bent over, pleading with him to stop.

But he has also seen her burst into tears just as quickly. One minute she's sweeping or cooking and then she stops and for no reason that he can see, she begins to cry.

The music stops and the news comes on. Usually he doesn't listen until the sports segment. But this newscaster is talking about fights that broke out at the Honvéd game yesterday afternoon. He's talking about hooligans and trouble-makers. The news surprises Tomi because when he and his father and Gabi listened to the game yesterday, the announcer didn't say anything about fighting. His mother shuts off the radio.

"But I want to hear."

"Come eat, boys," Emma-mama says, bringing in two bowls of carrot soup.

His mother signals Emma-mama to step outside. His ears perk up. Whenever his parents don't want him to hear, they send him out to play or they step into another room. So when they leave the room, Tomi, who always wants to know everything, listens.

"I don't like it."

Their voices are low. He has to strain to hear them.

"They're just hooligans."

"We've heard this before. These hooligans sing patriotic songs, recite patriotic poetry. You remember what followed last time."

"The Russians won't allow it."

"That's what those *smart* Jews said about the Guards of Silence when those rotten black-shirted Arrow-Cross animals roamed the streets. They said the Guards wouldn't let them hurt us and later those same *smart* Jews said they wouldn't let them take us. And where are those smart Jews now?"

"The Russians will protect us."

"No, they won't. Not if they don't see a good reason for themselves. You should have seen those patriots in the square this afternoon. They're this close to being a mob."

"I think you worry too much."

"I hope so, but I'll tell you one thing. I promised myself in Auschwitz that if I survived, I would never be a passive victim again! And no one, no one will harm my child because he's Jewish! Not while I'm alive. I swear I'll kill them with my bare hands if I have to."

He has never heard his mother talk like that. She is almost growling.

"Gabi, what's Auschwitz?"

Gabi, who is absorbed in looking at pictures of yesterday's game in *The People's Sports News*, doesn't answer.

"Gabi."

"What?" Gabi closes the paper and gets up.

"What's Auschwitz?"

"I don't know. Hurry up and finish your soup. The guys are waiting."

"Oh, yeah." Tomi, who likes to eat slowly and savour his food, drops his spoon and picks up the bowl. He slurps the rest of his soup and follows Gabi out the door.

"Where are you boys going?" Tomi's mother calls out after them.

"We're going to play soccer."

"No, you're not. Not today."

"Why not?" Gabi asks.

"Today is Chaider."

"And time for me to go back to work," Hannah says.

Hannah was a bookkeeper. When she applied for the job she knew nothing about it. She knew how to add, subtract, multiply and divide, but nothing about invoicing, debit, credit, payroll or how to calculate hourly wages in relationship to cubic feet of earth dug divided by collective teams of men working for the People's Water and Road Works. But she said she did. And she was hired because after the war there was a shortage of people who could do basic math and weren't Nazi sympathizers or collaborators. And there was pressure by the Communist party to hire Hungarians who had been in concentration camps as a visible reminder to those who had collaborated, to rub their noses in it. Hannah knew it and didn't mind that part one bit.

Hannah took home the books of her predecessor, an older man who had been the head bookkeeper until he was sent off to rehabilitation camp after it was discovered that he had been a bookkeeper in the Debrecen ghetto. Hannah pored over the books, trying to figure out how he got to the final numbers. She was working from solution to problem. She stayed up late, long after Tomi and Sanyi had gone to bed, tracking the steps like a hunter her prey. She was often frustrated, but that just made her more determined. It was more than the problem that drove her.

And when Hannah was singled out at a party meeting as an example of a good comrade, she put the commendation on the wall behind her desk so everyone who came to speak to her could see it and be afraid of her.

Often her colleagues would ask her for help but she mostly turned them down, claiming she wasn't a good teacher. Hannah was not eager to help those she held responsible, even if by their silence, for her mother's and sister's death. This made going to work pleasurable. The only one she helped was Berta, the chief of police's wife. She had learned from Magda in camp to cultivate only useful friends.

"Be careful," Emma-mama says, "and you boys go and get ready."

"Stupid Chaider," they grumble together.

"What's the point of learning Yiddish? Only old people like your grandfather and the rabbi speak it," Gabi says.

"And the alphabet is stupid," Tomi adds.

"Yeah, just a bunch of stupid doodles that you have to write backwards. So stupid."

—

The Kiosk is at the far end of the town square, a wooden structure not much bigger than their outhouse. The place is only big enough for Mrs. Tátra, her chair and her shelves of cigarettes, newspapers, and candy—Snowflakes, Snowballs, Turkish Delights, potato candy and Tomi's favourite, rock candy.

"Rock candy is a dangerous candy," his father had warned him the first time he bought him a coneful. "If you bite into it straight after putting it into your mouth, you can break a tooth. This is how you do it. First, you put it on your tongue like this," and stuck out his tongue and placed one on it." Tomi laughed. His father lifted it off his tongue and held it like a precious jewel. "Like a diamond on a velvet cushion. Slowly move your tongue around until its jagged edges round into a smooth little crystal soccer ball. This way it last longer and the sweetness spreads throughout your mouth."

Mrs. Tátra leans out her small window. "Ahh and what, as if I didn't know, would you boys like today?"

Before the boys can reply, three boys run up and shove Tomi and Gabi aside.

"Hey!" Gabi cries out. He recognizes Szeles.

"We want three cones of rock candies."

"Hey! We were here first!" Gabi says.

"So?" growls Szeles, who is half a head taller than Gabi.

"So, we were here first," Gabi says again.

"You want a slap in the head?" Szeles raises his palm. "Boys, I think he wants a slap in the head, what do you think?"

"Tibor Szeles, you and your friends wait your turn," Mrs. Tátra snaps. "They were here first."

Szeles makes a fist at Tomi and Gabi. "We'll get you," he mumbles under his breath as they line up behind them.

Tomi watches Mrs. Tátra as she folds a sheet of newspaper and tears it into quarters. She rolls two of them into ice cream-sized cones and fills them with rock candy.

Gabi pops one into his mouth and starts toward the synagogue. Tomi stops to look over his treasure. Each piece is a different shape, each no bigger than a pebble, and as hard as one. Some are clear as glass, others are milky. Choosing one is always an agonizing pleasure for him. He finally picks one, not the biggest but the shiniest. He holds it between his thumb and forefinger, feeling its sharp edges. Just as he is about to put it into his mouth, his head snaps forward and the cone flies out of his hand. The precious rocks rise into the air, hang suspended for an eternal moment, and then fall to the ground like shooting stars landing in the dust. He turns to see Szeles grinning wolfishly.

"You wanna do something about it?"

His eyes tear up.

"I dare you!"

Tomi clenches his fists. His jaw tightens.

"Come on, baby."

Mrs. Tátra pokes her head out the window. "What's going on out there?"

"The baby doesn't know how to hold his cone and spilled his candy," Szeles says.

She glares at Szeles and then at Tomi. "You have to be more careful," she says pulling her head like a turtle back inside the kiosk.

Tomi takes a deep breath to keep from crying. He unclenches his fists. Slowly he kneels to gather up his candy. Szeles shoves him and he loses his balance. The sharp edges of the candy scattered among the dirt and pebbles dig in like glass into his palms and knees.

"Ouch!" Tomi cries out.

"Be careful, baby." Szeles turns to his friends laughing. "The baby can't even walk yet."

By the time he hears Tomi's cry, Gabi is almost at the corner. When he turns around, he sees Tomi on all fours, picking up the candy. "No!" he yells, as he races back. He grabs Tomi by the wrist and yanks him upright. Tomi glares at Gabi while Gabi glares at Szeles.

"You wanna do something about it?"

Gabi presses his lips together. He clasps Tomi's hand and starts to pull him away but Tomi yanks his hand free. "Leave me alone."

Gabi extends his cone but Tomi shakes his head. Gabi takes one and gently places it into Tomi's raw and dirty palm and walks off. Tomi follows him. He can hear Szeles and his gang laughing. He looks back and sees Szeles and the others on their hands and knees, scooping up his candy from the dirt. He hates that they made him feel like a baby. Tomi didn't think Gabi would back down. He clenches his hands into fists. He can feel the sharp points of the candy Gabi gave him pierce his raw palm. He slips it into his pocket. He feels his penknife. He grasps it. Its knobby handle stings his palm. He wants to kill Szeles.

—

"Why do I have to go?" he asked his father when his parents first told him that he and Gabi would be going to Chaider.

"A long, long, long…"

"… time ago…"

"…when I was your age, I would go with my papa, may he rest in peace, to synagogue every Saturday to pray. The synagogue was so beautiful. Especially on the High Holidays. The women, including your grandmother, may she rest in peace, washed the floors so clean that you could eat off them. They cleaned the windows so clean that you'd swear that there was no glass in them. They polished the silver candelabras so bright that you didn't need candles in them. The men trimmed the lawn so fine that Puskás would have begged to play on it. And every year they gave the walls a new coat of yellow paint, so yellow that the sunflowers bowed their heads in their honour.

"I was so happy, standing next to Papa, listening to the Cantor sing the Kol Nidre. He sang it so beautifully. The notes rose like doves. They made you look up to the sky-blue dome with its sparkling golden stars and made you believe you were looking at the sky over Jerusalem, the real home of the Jews a long long long…"

"…time ago…"

"…And on Roshashona, all the Jews from the village and the surrounding farms came and filled the synagogue so full that you could not move. In those days, lots of Jewish families lived in and around Békes. Everyone was dressed in their New Year best. The girls came in their prettiest dresses and fanciest hats and the boys in their most starched and ironed shirts, finest holiday suits and spit-and-polish boots. My sister, your Aunt Margit, and I were also there in our best patched hand-me-downs."

"Why were you so poor?"

"God knows. Somebody had to be rich, somebody had to be poor. We were the Chosen. But we weren't the only ones. There were enough of us poor to form our own congregation if we had wanted to. I loved Yom Kippur. I was happy on Yom Kippur because it was the one day a year we were equal to every other Jewish family. It's, as you know, the one day when everybody has to fast, not just the poor. On that day, on the Day of Atonement, everybody goes without food. And as much as I loved hearing the shofar end the fast, I was sad because the rich with their overflowing larders always went home to eat a big, big, big meal while we only had chicken soup without the chicken.

"But we were proud to be Hajdú Jews. For us, it wasn't the Hajdús who made Békes famous. For us it was our synagogue and Rabbi Stern, your Rabbi Stern's father, may he rest in peace. When he gave his sermon, it was so quiet you could hear a leaf fall. He was also renowned and respected for his wisdom. People would come from all over Hungary to ask our rabbi for advice. Even other rabbis. Even the gentiles. Imagine! Families from all over Hungary sent their sons to study with him. Even from Budapest. There were so many students that a big classroom had to be built. I wanted to go to Chaider and hear what he had to say and maybe become a wise rabbi, but we were too poor. And then the war happened. But now you have a chance to learn from his son, who is also wise. So I want you to go, listen and learn so you can grow up to be a wise man. A wise man is a rich man. And that kind of wealth nobody can take away from you."

—

The synagogue is kitty-corner to his real school and almost as big. But large plaster chunks of the synagogue's exterior walls are strewn like crushed clouds on the weed-ridden lawn. The cracked windowpanes are caked with dirt and the ones without glass are criss-crossed by fly-filled spider webs. Tomi, Gabi and their friends sometimes sneak in and play among the overturned pews, hunt mice and rats as they scurry in and out of the bullet-riddled ark where the Torah used to be and use the stained-glass Star of David above it and the faded gold stars on the dome the boys call the "Jew hat" as targets for their slingshot competitions. Until Rabbi Stern comes running to chase them away.

"Why do we have to waste our time learning about people with stupid names like Ezekiel, Ishmael and Nebuchadnezzar who lived a long, long, long time ago in far, far, far, faraway places that don't exist anymore? I don't want to be a rabbi. I want to be like Puskás."

"And I want to be like Grosics. Especially this afternoon."

It's going to be Tomi's first game on the school field, his first game with real nets. "Yeah. Stupid Chaider," Tomi says as he puts on his yarmulke. He hadn't heard Rabbi Stern come up behind and is taken by surprise when the rabbi slaps him on the back of the head.

"Ouch."

"It's you who are stupid," the rabbi says and shepherds the boys into the classroom. "Now sit and try to learn something." It's the second time Tomi has been slapped on the back of the head today. He wants to slap somebody.

Rabbi Stern is about the same size as Small Potato. His dark eyes can burn holes into his students when he looks at them. His fiery cheeks are always flushed. He has a thick moustache, a large bushy beard and smelly tobacco breath.

Chaider classes are held in Rabbi Stern's house next to the old synagogue. During the week, the dining room serves as the classroom and on Saturdays and High Holidays it becomes the synagogue. It has a low ceiling with small windows that makes the room dark no matter what time of day it is. He keeps the Torah in the cupboard.

Each class begins with a recitation of the Hebrew alphabet. Holding a cigarette between his fingers, waving it like a baton, Rabbi Stern keeps time. As he does, he circles the table, palm at the ready for a quick slap on the back of the head to any boy who mispronounces or doesn't know the letters. Both Tomi and Gabi have been recipients of such slaps. But often it's Yossel, the rabbi's own son, the only one besides Rabbi Stern with earlocks and who always wears a yarmulke and a tzitzit, who gets the most and hardest whacks, even though he hardly makes any mistakes.

Yossel is reading, "And I am come down to deliver them out of the land of the Egyptians, and to bring them up out of that land unto a good land and a large one, unto a land flowing with milk and honey, unto the place of the Canaanite, and Hittite and the Amorite and the Perizzite, and the Jebusite," when Gabi puts up his hand.

The rabbi, pleased, nods. "Yes?"

"I have to go to the bathroom."

He glares at Gabi. "Sit down."

Gabi squeezes his knees together. He pinches his face into a look of desperation. "But Rabbi, I really have to go."

The rabbi shakes his head with displeasure. He doesn't want to let him out but he also doesn't want an accident in his class. "So, you couldn't go before? Your bladder is suddenly like the walls of Jericho, about to burst?" He heaves a sigh. "So go, but hurry back."

"Yes, Rabbi," Gabi says and hurries out.

"So continue," he commands his son with a whack on the head. He ambles back to his stuffed fauteuil and sits, interlocking his fingers over his stomach. He leans back, closes his eyes and listens as Yossel continues his reading.

As soon as Tomi hears the first audible snores, he quietly slides off the bench and tiptoes toward the door. The other boys watch as he slowly opens it, trying to keep it from creaking. Yossel smiles at him and continues reading his passage, a bit louder. Tomi smiles back and eases out, closing the door quietly behind him.

Outside, he runs toward the outhouse, which, like most, is located as far away from the main house as possible. The Chaider's smelly fly-infested outhouse is next to the chicken coop and across the lane from the school. He ducks behind it.

He can hear the shouts of Carrot, Frog, István, Gabi and the other regulars. He squeezes through the broken slats of the fence, and runs across the alley to join them on the field.

—

"Everybody knows that Puskás is the best forward in the world," Tomi says.

"I like Kocsis," Frog says.

"He's not the captain of Honvéd."

"Kocsis is the best header in the world."

"Puskás is also the captain of the national team. And the Olympic team. And they won the gold medal."

"Kocsis can do the best scissors kicks."

"Puskás can blast goals from the 16-metre line and he can hit the pigeonholes blindfolded. That's what I want to do."

Gyuri, the star of Békes's team, has been helping Tomi develop his accuracy, showing him how to get his toes under the ball, spread his arms to keep possession of it, lean back to control the height, and get the most power into his shots.

"Most important," he tells Tomi, "you have to believe that you can shoot it where you want it. Picture it in your mind and tell yourself that you can do it."

"You and Gabi are going to be very good players. And if you keep practising you're going to be on the county junior team," Coach Varga keeps telling them at each practice.

Gabi's hero is Grosics, The Black Panther, who is the best goalie in the world. Gabi loves imitating his leaps and can already make it halfway across the net.

Gabi is always captain of the Hungarian side, which also includes Tomi, Carrot and István. Frog is captain of the other team. He and the other Gypsy boys are always whatever team Honvéd last played. Before the game begins, Frog and his teammates, who play barefoot, clear off the larger pieces of gravel that are scattered about the field.

"Gypsies are poor," Tomi's mother explained to him when she wouldn't let him run barefoot like Frog. "And they like running around barefoot. It comes naturally to them. They only wear shoes in winter and on special occasions."

Tomi and Gabi wear their itchy special sweaters that Tomi's Aunt Margit sent from Canada.

"She left right after the war, before you were born," his father told him.

"Why?" Tomi asked.

"She didn't want to stay in Hungary anymore."

"Why not?" He couldn't understand why someone wouldn't want to live in Hungary.

"She lives in Montreal."

"Where's that?

"In Canada."

"Where is that?"

"In America."

"In America? Are there cowboys and Indians where she lives? Does she ride horses and shoot Indians? Can we visit her?"

He wonders if she's rich. He has heard his parents talk about people in America being rich. "Everybody has a car," his father says." Aunt Margit must be rich because she has her own restaurant and twice a year his father would arrive home from the post office with a bulging pillowcase from her.

And whenever his father returned with the pillowcase, neighbours and acquaintances would start dropping by to say hello and to complain that they had recently been to the People's Haberdashery to look for a shirt for their husbands, or a pair of shorts for their boys, or a blouse for themselves or their daughters but couldn't find anything worth spending their hard-earned money on. Wasn't it a shame, they said, that they had the money but the store didn't have the goods.

"Nice of them all to just drop by. What a coincidence that they came today," Dezső-papa always remarked after they left.

"Yes, it is. They're very good neighbours that way," Tomi's father said every time.

After supper on these occasions, they always gathered in their bedroom-sitting room where the bulging pillowcase lay on the bed like a stuffed goose. The ritual was always the same. He and Gabi would sit on their fathers' laps and watch Tomi's mother carefully untie the string and give it to Emma, who would roll it into a ball that she tucked into her apron pocket. After Hannah carefully unstitched the sewn end of the pillow, she reached in and drew out a piece of clothing and held it up for all to see. Turning it front to back, the mothers oohed and aahhed and then laid it delicately like a newborn onto the bed. He and Gabi were always hoping for toys or books but were usually disappointed because Auntie Margit, being a grown-up and unmarried, didn't think of sending anything besides "stupid old clothes."

When Tomi complained, his mother always told him, "Be thankful. It's because of Auntie Margit that you have such nice clothes. Even if they're not new, they're nicer and better than what anybody else has."

"They're even better and nicer than what you can get in Budapest," Emma-mama always said. The clothes that didn't fit, Tomi's mother could usually alter and those that they didn't want they could easily sell to those who dropped by. And those too worn or with holes in them she would give to Frog's mother in exchange for doing the laundry.

"Now comes the treasure hunt," Dezső-papa would say once everything was laid out on the bed.

"Why does she hide stuff?" Gabi once asked.

"Because the customs officers, those honourable comrade protectors of Hungary's purity, inspect everything to make sure that no capitalist propaganda or money is smuggled in. Of course, while they're protecting us from capitalism, they steal whatever they can. I bet they won't teach you that in Little Drummers," he said to Gabi.

"Dezső, don't say such things. The walls have ears."

Dezső-papa just waved his hand like he was brushing away a fly and drank another shot of pálinka. "Somebody has to tell them the truth." Then he turned to the wall and said, "You hear? Yes, *you*, walls with ears!"

He liked it when Gabi's father said things like that. It was funny. He could imagine walls with ears.

His mother slowly and thoroughly patted the linings of the sleeves and the shoulder paddings of the most tattered jackets.

"Why there?" Gabi had asked.

"Because Auntie Margit knows those bright customs men don't bother with the jackets that are old and worn. They don't think they have any value. So that's where she hides those seamless nylons and American dollars," Dezsö-papa said.

Tomi didn't understand why seamless nylons were so valuable but he knew the girls and women who visited his parents always oohed and aahed about them.

These parcels made Tomi's and Gabi's family different from the other families. His mother appreciated quality and she loved to wear nice clothes. Sometimes she would stand in front of the mirror for a long time trying on the garments Auntie Margit sent, turning slowly and looking at herself, tugging and tucking until she was satisfied and then she would smile. She also made sure that he and his father went to the Sunday soccer games in their American clothes.

"I like it when the women compliment me on my clothes. I can see their envy dripping like bacon fat," he had heard his mother say after one of their Sunday walks.

The two sweaters were at the bottom of the last parcel. They were red. Tomi and Gabi could hardly believe their eyes! They leaped off their fathers' laps like cats who had seen mice and grabbed them from their mothers' hands. Two thin white bands ran across the middle. Between them was a wide blue band with a crest on the front. The letter 'C' looked like a horseshoe and had an H inside of it.

"Look! 'H' for Honvéd."

"It almost looks like a Honvéd sweater!"

"They even have numbers on the back!"

Both were number nine. And though it wasn't Puskás's number ten, it *was* a number. None of the kids in town had a sweater with a number. No one had anything like these. They pressed them to their chests almost simultaneously. Furiously, they pulled and wiggled the sweaters over their heads. They were a little tight and itchy, smelled of mothballs and had a few small holes in the shoulders and the sleeves.

"They're great," Gabi said.

"They're perfect," Tomi shouted.

———

Tomi has scored a couple of Puskás-like goals and Gabi has made a couple of his Grosics panther-leap saves. His team is leading when Szeles and his gang shows up. They stop at the touchline and watch.

István lobs a pass towards Tomi for a head and run. As he speeds toward it, looking up at the ball, Tomi feels a foot across his ankle, and suddenly he is tumbling. He hears laughing. He looks up and sees Szeles with one foot on the ball, arms crossed, grinning like a warrior chief who has conquered an opponent.

"The baby still can't walk. We're gonna play. You Jewboys can even have those stinking Gypsies on your team." He flashes a mean-looking smile. Tomi knows there is no choice about letting them play.

Szeles and his gang play rough and dirty. They shove, elbow, and deliberately step on the Gypsy boys' bare feet. Only Gabi's brilliant goaltending keeps them in the game.

Frog has the ball at mid-field. Just before getting knocked over, he passes the ball to Carrot who sends a lead pass to Tomi. He takes it on his instep and dribbles over to the right side. He sees Szeles charging.

"Jew! Jew! Jews eat dirt!" Szeles shouts as he gallops towards Tomi.

"You can do it. You can do it." He can see Szeles's mean eyes glowing and his wide grin and big teeth. Tomi spreads his arms, leans back as if he were flying, gets his foot under the ball and kicks it as hard as he can. Szeles rises onto his toes, his eyes widen and a high-pitched yelp escapes from his gaping mouth. He is still and stiff as a statue. Then in one motion his knees buckle, his hands grasp his groin, and he falls face down onto the ground with a thud. He lies there. Tomi is scared. Maybe he killed him. Everybody gathers round Szeles. After what seems like forever, slowly he rolls over onto his back. He lies there; hands at his groin, eyes and mouth wide open, desperately trying to breathe. A loud sob escapes from his mouth, a gob of snot flies from his nose and lands in his mouth.

"You did that on purpose!" yells one of Szeles's gang and takes a step toward Tomi. Tomi stiffens and clenches his fists.

Just then a throaty burp startles everyone into silence. Something flies out of Frog's pocket. It makes a beautiful arc through the air before landing smack in the middle of Szeles's face.

"Get it off of me!" Szeles croaks, slapping at his own face.

Even Szeles's friends laugh.

"Tamás, Gábor!" The angry voice cuts through the yelling and laughing. Everyone turns. It's Rabbi Stern standing on the other side of the fence, by the outhouse, wagging his finger at them.

"You get back here right now!"

—

Tomi loves Sundays. He can stay in his pyjamas longer and his parents don't have to go to work. Nobody is rushing him to finish breakfast. Also it's the one day that his mother does the cooking. During the week, because she doesn't work, it's Emma-mama who cooks, but on Sunday his mother takes over the kitchen. In the summer, she usually makes cold fruit soups and chicken paprika. In the fall, it's usually goulash. Both Emma-mama and his mother are good cooks but he prefers his mother's cooking because it's hers. After every Sunday noon meal his father put his hands on his full stomach, like the pashas Tomi has seen in books, and declares that his wife is the best cook not only because she cooks so well but because she makes a lot. Of course Dezsö-papa also says the same thing about Emma-mama's cooking.

"To make up for all the ones we missed," is his mother's regular reply.

Sunday afternoons after the meal, before the game on the radio, his father and Deszö-papa have a shot of pálinka and usually take their naps on the verandah. Emma-mama tends her roses or listens to the music on the radio. For his mother, Sunday afternoons are a time for reading. She says that it is like going to other times and other countries. Her favourite book is *Les Misérables* and the poems of Petőfi Sándor.

Tomi and Gabi practise what Coach Varga taught them that week. Today Gabi is throwing the ball into the air, making Tomi leap as high as he can to head it back. Tomi tries to angle the headers to the corners so Gabi can practise his leaps.

There is a knock at the front door.

"Who disturbs the peace?" Gabi's father shouts, rousing from his nap. "Don't they know it's Sunday?"

Tomi's father gets up and goes to the door. He returns with Rabbi Stern.

The boys stop their practice when they see the rabbi on the verandah. Although he's dressed in his usual black suit and hat, he looks more serious than he does in school. The rabbi looks at the boys, who stand still, waiting to be called.

Tomi's father disappears into the house.

"Please sit. Would you like a cup of tea?" his mother asks.

"No, thank you." The rabbi remains standing.

"A shot of pálinka?" Gabi's father asks, pouring himself another.

"No, thank you," he says a bit more hesitantly.

Tomi sees Dezsö-papa is smiling. His mother told Tomi after one of Rabbi Stern's visits that the rabbi doesn't eat or drink at other people's houses because most Jews no longer keep a kosher home.

Tomi's father returns wearing a yarmulke. Gabi's father looks at him and snorts. "Ah. Found your religion, Sanyi? Was it next to the pork chops?"

Tomi and Gabi look at each other. They know why the rabbi is here. He's been here before to complain about their behaviour and truancy.

"What do you expect? They're boys. Boys like to play, not study things that are of no use to them," Gabi's father says loudly.

"So it's from you they get those ideas. If it's useless, then why do you send them?" The rabbi's voice also rises.

"Ask my wife. She's the one who insists."

"Then she's the wise one in your family. Learning your people's language and history and praying to God is of no use? It's a sin to talk like that."

"Don't you wag your finger at me, Rabbi! Tell me, what has all this learning and sticking to our tradtion got us? Look around. You see every day from your window how His house looks. How His house was looted; the doors and the benches chopped up, carried off for firewood, His crystal chandeliers, brass door plates and handles pillaged, and His holy books burned. And look around. Count how many of His people returned to this miserable little village and count how many didn't."

The rabbi lifts his head to the sky. "God has His reasons."

"Then let's hear them. Don't you think it's about time?"

"Dezsö!" Gabi's mother pleads. "Have respect. He's a rabbi."

"Why? God doesn't. How come God doesn't respect him? If he's so close to God, how come God treated him so badly? How come He didn't spare his wife and daughter?"

"Dezsö!" Gabi's and his mother cry out.

There's silence. This is not what Tomi expected. He's never heard anybody yell at the Rabbi. You're supposed to respect the teacher.

Rabbi Stern takes a deep breath and raises his eyes to the sky. "God's ways are mysterious. We are just ordinary mortals who can't understand His ways. Ours is not to question but to obey and study the Torah and wait for The Messiah."

"Look what studying the Torah got us. And waiting for the Messiah? Well, if Auschwitz and all the other camps weren't the right time for Him to send The Messiah, then I'm afraid of what will have to happen for it to be the right time."

"We are his Chosen People. He will take care of us."

"He sure hasn't so far, has He? I think it's time for us to take care of ourselves."

"And how do you do that? By changing your name, making it sound less Jewish, more Christian?"

"Yes, I changed the family name. I did it for my son, so he won't face the same hatred that we did."

"And look what difference it makes. He's still being called a dirty Jew. You can give up your earlocks, tallis, and even change your name, but people still know who and what you are. You think by assimilating you're solving the problem? Is this how you remember and honour your mother and father and brothers and sisters who were murdered? Look, Dezsö, you and Sanyi are good people, good Jews, there are no other kind. Teach your sons to respect their heritage; tell them what happened so they will remember."

"We will tell them what they need to know when we think they are ready," Tomi's father says, as he turns to call the boys.

"Let them be. Don't tell them to apologize to me. Tell them to apologize to God. And maybe you should too," the rabbi says, looking Dezsö-papa straight in the eyes before turning to leave.

OCTOBER

·

1956

4

As the buyer for The People's Hardware of Békes, Sanyi travels to Budapest four times a year. Hannah always accompanies him to the train station to see him off. They call it their Budapest Stroll.

Walking arm in arm down Market Street, Sanyi smiles at everyone they meet, remembering that there was a time, not so long ago, when he wasn't even allowed to walk on this street. Now as they promenade, he makes sure that he hesitates just long enough before nodding so that it is they who nod first. He wants to feel like he owns the street. When he looks at his wife, he smiles, and knows that with her on his arm he does.

He remembers how resentful his co-workers were when he was given a job. He overheard them whispering to each other 'It's because he's a Jew. They gave it to him to punish us.' He was scared at first and happy to hide in the basement stocking shelves and sweeping. Then Hannah's father had a word with him.

When Moses Schwartz spoke, you listened. After all, when he got back and found his neighbours living in his house, hadn't he threatened to go to the liberating Russians and report them as collaborators if they weren't out by nightfall? And hadn't he been through two world wars and the White Terror pogroms? He had lost his wife and youngest child, but still believed in God and a future. "Only worms and the dead live underground," he told Sanyi. "You're not a worm, you are a man and you're alive. You survived. God has plans for you."

After his talk with Moses, Sanyi thought differently. He worked hard. He was a fast learner and organized. And now he was the store's buyer. Who would have thought that the constant yelling by the rotten guards—"Quick, everything and everyone in their place! Or else!"— and the beatings would help him to succeed. But now people don't just whisper. They say it louder, like before, that it's because of the Jews that they're having trouble. They yearn for the good old days.

Sanyi, like every other Jew who survived, is scarred by the war. His wounds aren't physical or visible. Those healed. The deep wounds are to his soul. They're in his spirit, festering. Some survivors sank into a dark world of silence, and others talked about nothing else. Sanyi covers up his pain with an outward respectfulness and friendliness. He compliments his boss, whom he had seen before the war wearing the Arrow-Cross armband, on his fine shirts. He acts friendly with the customers who tell him anti-Semitic jokes, but he takes pleasure in shortchanging them as he distracts them with jokes of his own or slips his thumb on the scale as he weighs their purchases.

"The People's Hardware belongs to the people," is what Árpád says at the start of every Party meeting of the hardware store. "We work for them. We make sure that everybody gets his fair share. Helping the people get their fair share is the goal of the Party and we who work here. And to achieve this goal we need to work hard."

"Ha. The only thing everybody gets a fair share of is nothing. Nobody, not even Comrade Commissar Árpád, believes it," Sanyi tells Hannah after these meetings. "I know because many times I've had him on my 'real' list. Fair share depends on who you know and how good a wheeler-dealer you are."

Sanyi is a good wheeler-dealer. He uses his Charlie Chaplin smile and self-deprecating humour to convince whomever he's dealing with that he's an easy mark, someone they can take advantage of. Letting the other buyers think they're getting the better deal is an art he has mastered well. He enjoys playing the game because he always wins. For him it is a serious game. He mastered it in the camps. He had to. It was the difference between starving and eating, living and dying. Losing meant death.

Hannah is a petite woman. Though she only comes up a little past Sanyi's shoulders, farm life and Auschwitz have toughened her. Since her return she always walks with purpose and strength. Her dark brown eyes glow with harsh defiance, especially when she walks with her husband.

Today, she is wearing a bright headscarf with vivid red maple leaves that shows off her black shoulder-length hair and a skirt she made out of material that Margit sent. She takes pride in the seamstress skills her mother taught her, and with the fine scissors and sewing machine Sanyi wheeled and dealt for her, she tailors her clothes better than the town's seamstress. They are always a fine fit. This smart houndstooth outfit is eye-catching. Its waist is neatly tucked; the calf-length hem is even and sharply ironed. It accents her figure. She knows it. And with her seamless nylons, she knows that she is the envy of the women they meet. And she is glad.

Everybody in Békes knows when Sanyi is off to Budapest. Men begin to drop into the store a few days before he is due to leave. They complain about what the store never has or carries enough of and let him know that they wouldn't mind paying a little extra to get it. He listens respectfully and nods. Sanyi always goes to Budapest with two lists: the People's Hardware list and what he calls "the real people's" list.

"All aboard!"

Although Sanyi likes Budapest, he doesn't like leaving Hannah and Tomi. Even for a day or two. It's a survivor's fear. Hannah is his love, his reason for not giving up. And his son is his personal victory and the future he is working for. He holds his wife close. Finally, reluctantly, he boards the train. A shrill hiss of steam and a dark cloud of smoke spews from the engine's stack. The train lurches forward.

"I'll be back by Friday."

"Don't forget to talk to Ernö!"

He stands on the steps of the moving train, one hand gripping the handrail, the other waving.

Hannah doesn't wave back. She stands motionless as the train curves slowly around the bend and disappears into the early light of the October morning.

———

Sanyi gazes out the train window. The colours of summer are gone. The harvest is over. The lushness of corn and sunflower fields has given way to grey and clumpy vistas. Only the occasional solitary leafless tree interrupts the flatness.

"Hajdúszabad," the conductor calls out. Every time the train stops here, Sanyi feels a crowd of memories get on board. He was twenty-two in 1943 when he was conscripted and sent here with all the other able-bodied Jewish men from around the county. Although they were officially in the army, they weren't issued weapons or trained for combat. Instead, they were given picks, shovels and brooms. And instead of participating in manoeuvres, they dug ditches, repaired roads and cleaned the camp: the officers' mess, the yard and the latrines.

One morning the camp sergeant of his platoon called for volunteers who could sing. Sanyi, who had a good voice, was tempted, thinking that this might be a soft assignment. He thought that he might get to sing in the officers' mess and get to eat their leftovers or be assigned to an officer. But he had been warned by older conscripts never to volunteer. A young red-haired, rosy-cheeked boy stepped forward.

"Let's hear you sing," the sergeant ordered the young boy.

He sang, Sanyi still remembers, a popular plaintive song of the time about a young man asking a little bird to carry his love to his beloved.

"You," the sergeant barked, after the boy finished, "will climb this tree every morning before sunrise and you will crow like a rooster to rouse all these lazy Jews!"

Sanyi was assigned to the bakery. He rose even before "Red Rooster"—as the boy in the tree was nicknamed—and spent most of his days carrying fifty-kilo bags of flour, chopping wood, kneading dough and standing in front of a blazing oven. It was hard and sweaty work in summer, but in winter when his fellow conscripts were shivering all day, he was warm. It also gave him the opportunity to do a little wheeling and dealing. His sergeant liked to smoke, but cigarettes were in short supply. Sanyi told him that he might be able to get him some tobacco for some buns and permission to say a prayer over the dough every morning.

The more religious the conscript, the dirtier the job he got. The Hassidic boys were usually given the dirtiest. They had latrine duty and yard clean up. They always smelled of excrement. In the morning, they cleaned the latrines and in the afternoon, on all fours and with just their bare hands, they were forced to sweep the yard clean, which included dog, chicken and bird droppings. It was demeaning, but the Hassids managed to turn it to their advantage by collecting the guards' and officers' discarded cigarette butts. And at night, before lights out, as they gathered for evening prayers in their bunks, while praying, they unrolled the butts and gave Sanyi the gathered tobacco. After taking a little for himself, he gave the rest to the sergeant in charge of the bakery who in return gave him cigarette papers, let him pray over the dough and sneak some buns.

His prayer over the dough made the buns kosher enough for the Hassidic boys and kept them from starving. It was one of the few things in their meagre rations that they could eat. Every night, the boys blessed him for it. Sanyi smiled to himself whenever he thought about his labour camp wheelings and dealings, how the discarded scraps of their tormentors turned into earthly treasure, pleasures, the staff of life and heavenly blessings.

The train jerks forward again. The large tracts of grey harvested fields of the collective farms give way to villages, towns and cities. Sanyi looks over his inventory list. It includes the usual: axe and hammer heads, saws, iron bars, clamps, rolls of wire, bicycle inner tubes, balls of twine and heavy rope. His "real people's list," the one he kept in his head, has on it three iron cauldrons, an electric iron, a stove and two boys' bicycles. Most of these items are still hard to come by, even unofficially. But Sanyi is determined to get them. Success is the salve that eases his deepest pains.

———

Whenever he's in Budapest, Sanyi goes for breakfast at The Golden Bull Café with Ernő Lakatos, the chief manager of The People's Central Hardware Warehouse. It was Ernő who introduced Sanyi to the expensive and exclusive bistro frequented by the important people of the Communist Party.

Sanyi loves having breakfast at The Golden Bull. He always orders the same thing and goes through the same ritual. He closes his eyes and inhales deeply, savouring the aromatic rising steam of real coffee. Real coffee, like seamless nylons, is a luxury, very expensive and almost impossible to come by. Even he has trouble getting it. Most restaurants serve chicory, a bitter and woody substitute.

Once his nostrils fill with the aroma of coffee, he opens his eyes and takes his slice of the fresh rye bread, tears off a piece and dips it into the coffee, slowly and gently, as if he were baptizing a baby. Reverently, he raises the coffee-soaked bread to his lips, slips it into his mouth and closes his eyes. He squeezes it between his tongue and the roof of his mouth until the bread-filtered coffee fills his palate. He lets the coffee glide down his throat slowly. And then, only then, does he thoroughly chew and swallow the coffee-flavoured piece of bread. "This way," Sanyi smiles and explains to Ernö, "both the bread and coffee are doubly delicious."

"You really like your food," Ernö said, when he watched Sanyi's ritual for the first time.

"You know the saying 'at breakfast, eat like a king, at noon, like a man and at night, like a beggar'? Well, when I was young, we were very poor, so I had no trouble following the supper advice of these wise words. It was the morning and noon parts that I had trouble with. So now, when I can, I try to make amends and try to fully obey the commandments of eating as a king and as a man."

"Very wise of you, Sanyi, very wise." Ernö laughs.

Sanyi not only pays for Ernö's breakfast but also always brings him a gift. Sometimes it's a pair of nylons or a bottle of homemade pálinka. "Winter's coming. The farmers say it's going to be a hard one. They say that their winter salami will be in great demand. Even though I'm forbidden to eat it, I love that pork meat spiced with white pepper, cured in the cold air, smoked slowly and aged for a year. Don't you? And the great thing about it is that you can keep it for a long time and it won't go bad. They tell me that most of it has already been exported and they'll be hard to get even in those Party member shops. And even there, they'll be expensive. I figure at least my month's salary. But I managed to get one rod for you. So here, enjoy."

"Thanks, it's appreciated. My mother loves it," Ernö smiles as he slips it into his briefcase.

"How is your dear mother?"

"She's fine, and once she sees this gift, she'll be even better. You should come and visit sometime."

"Thank you for the invitation. My family and I would like to."

"Christmas is coming soon. Now tell me, what do you want Santa to bring you?"

Today, Sanyi is negotiating with Ernö for something more than the usual stuff. He knows the salami will help. It's worth the expense. Besides, he isn't the one paying for it. It's the cost of doing business which he passes on to those on his "real people's list."

Sanyi turns toward the growing noise coming from the square across the street. "How is it going?" he asks.

Ernö glances out the window at the large crowd gathered in Red Square.

"They're getting bigger every day."

"What do they want?"

"Change," Ernö replies, sipping his coffee.

"To me, it looks like they want trouble. Smaller but similar gatherings are going on these days in Békes. Who are they?"

"Mainly students. They want freedom of speech and reform of what they think is a corrupt system and government. Now they're calling on the factory workers and the farmers to join them. They're even asking the army to join them."

Sanyi had felt this same kind of fervour and heard this kind of talk before the war. He can smell trouble the way he can smell the coffee he's sipping. Except that the coffee has a pleasant aroma.

"And you?" he asks. "You went to Karl Marx University. What do you think?"

"The system is good. It's the bureaucrats and the leaders. The system is like a garden; it needs weeding or the weeds will choke the flowers. The problem is that the weeds are in power. So it's like asking the weeds to weed themselves." He stares into his coffee.

"The demonstrators are idealists and dreamers. We need dreamers."

"They may be dreamers here, but in Békes," Sanyi says, lowering his voice and leaning close, "they make nightmares. This is not a good time to be a Jew. Again."

A silence settles between them.

"Sanyi, I've heard of people, mostly your kind, who are planning to leave."

Sanyi turns his gaze back to the crowd in Red Square. Some are wearing armbands, reminding him of just before the war when the Arrow Cross Blackshirts gathered in Békes's town square, demanding a pure Hungary. He takes a deep breath. "How are they planning to leave?"

Ernö leans in and lowers his voice. "Well, I've heard that there are people who will guide them across the border into Austria."

Sanyi looks him in the eye. "Do you know any such people?"

Ernö took a sip of his coffee and calmly looks around. "How many stoves do you want?"

Sanyi hesitates for a minute. "Three. Two damaged, you know the kind, with bits of ceramic paint chipped off, and a small new one."

Ernö gives him the price.

"That's high."

"The demand is high. It's supply and demand," he says, turning to look at the overflowing crowd.

5

"I'm no longer the buyer for the store," Sanyi announces on the night of his return from Budapest. "I've been demoted to the stock room. Gyuri, that peasant who barely knows how to write his name, and who *I* hired so he could play for the team, reported me."

"Gyuri showed me a new move!"

"That louse. From now on you're not to play with him!"

"Why not?"

"Because I say so!"

Tomi's father has never yelled at him before.

"Your father isn't angry at you. Go clean your bike and put it in the shed. Then I'll help you practise your poem."

"You too, Gabi," Emma-mama says.

"Can I ride it?"

"No! Just put it in the shed!" His father bangs his fist on the table.

"Sanyi!" His mother yells at his father.

"Go on, boys," Dezsö-papa says quietly.

Wordlessly, they head for the verandah, where their bikes are leaning against the wall. He doesn't understand why his father is so angry at him. He stops outside the door to listen.

"Did you get caught *stealing*?"

"No! The idiot finally learned to count and reported to the party secretary that we had more stock than what was on the inventory list. Imagine! I get demoted because there is *more!*"

"The police have been called in. Berta told me. She said that Laci was told to investigate."

"Laci and Berta, friends. Some friends. Because of me, they have a brand new stove. They'd be waiting for years if I hadn't made a side deal. And now *he's* going to arrest me."

Tomi is scared. Is his father going to be put in jail??

"It's not Laci's fault. Berta told me that Laci said that he could delay the investigation for a little while. He suggested that this would be a good time for us to go visit relatives in Sopron."

"What relatives?" Tomi asks from the verandah. He doesn't know of any relatives living in Sopron.

"We'll tell you later, Elephant Ears," his mother calls back. "Now finish cleaning your bike and get ready for bed."

The adults lower their voices, and now he can't make out what they are saying.

Reluctantly, he joins Gabi, who is already wiping the spokes. When Tomi's father had surprised them with the bikes, he could hardly believe his eyes. Two Superlas. None of the other kids in town had one. "I wanted you and Gabi to have something brand new when you started school. It's a bit late but not too late," his father said when he showed up with them.

The bikes are shiny blood-red, like the star above the blackboard at school. Every night after supper, before locking them up, the boys clean the spokes, mudguards and rims. They use axle grease from the blacksmiths to lubricate the chains and keep them rust-free. With extra care they polish the chrome handlebars and buff the silvery Superla logo.

But tonight, Tomi is more interested in his parents' conversation than cleaning his bike. He's scared. He has never seen his father like this. He and Gabi lock up their bikes.

Gabi goes inside, but Tomi doesn't feel like getting ready for bed. He lingers next to the kitchen door. Even though it's chilly he stands without moving a muscle, listening.

"The leadership '*asked*' me to step down as manager of the team," his father says.

Why would they ask his father to quit? Everybody likes him. At games people are always coming up to him, always joking with him, praising him for getting good players for the team. And even though he doesn't play on the team, they say that he is part of the team. If his father's no longer allowed to be part of the team, how will Tomi be able to practise with them and learn new tricks? It's not fair.

Tomi's father is passionate about Hajdubékes's team. His mother told him of the time, before he was born, she'd sent his father out to buy some butter and on the way to the store, the team bus came by. The fans were on their way to Dobos for a game. Without hesitation, Sanyi jumped on board.

"He came home after supper all excited about the win," Tomi's mother had said. "When I asked him about the butter, he looked at me as if I was speaking Turkish."

Before the war, Sanyi was crazy about soccer. Even in the early days of labour camp, even after a day of heavy labour, when they were given a bit of free time, he was always eager to play a pickup game. But the concentration camp killed his passion for most things, including soccer. Soccer was something that belonged to his youth and the camp had stolen that from him.

He and his sister Margit were the only survivors of their family. Margit came back hating the country and the people who allowed this to happen to her and her family. She was determined to leave. She begged Sanyi to go with her while it was still possible. Sanyi didn't have the will. He had no desire to move. He felt too empty to make an effort at living again. It was easier to do what he had learned to do at the camp—follow orders and go through the motions. It was easier than starting again.

The job at The People's Hardware Store allowed him to spend his days alone in the basement stockroom, stacking, organizing and cleaning. After his time in the crowded camp, in the overcrowded bunkhouse, he wanted to be left alone and unseen. He felt safe in that damp underground. Only once a week, on market days, did he venture out from the stockroom.

Moses Schwartz came to Békes on market days. He usually brought his daughter Hannah along to help him at his stall. Sanyi would walk over during his lunch break and sit silently while he ate the food that Hannah had brought him. Then, he'd nod and walk back to the store.

Both Hannah and Sanyi were survivors. Both shared the loss of their youth. They felt the emptiness and the guilt of having survived while their mothers, brothers and sisters hadn't. They shared the knowledge that nothing could make the void disappear. But sitting there, eating in silence, they also shared an unspoken feeling that together it might be easier. And as spring follows winter, so the ice in Sanyi's soul began to melt and feelings slowly started to come back to life. Sanyi fell in love again.

Moses encouraged him to think of the future. "Don't forget the past—we can't, we mustn't—but look to the future because *that* is where you are going to be," Moses instructed him. "And I want my son-in-law to be a husband that my daughter and I can be proud of."

After they married and settled in his parents' old house, Hannah began to encourage him to attend soccer games even though he was no longer interested in soccer. One Sunday afternoon, trying to convince him, she said, "If you don't go, then who's going to take your son?"

"If...what? Really?"

Soccer became part of his life again. Life became a part of him too. At first he sat apart from the crowd, detached, blankly watching the young men running about on the field aimlessly as though the game was being played in a fog. All motion seemed to be ghostly grey. It had no shape. But imperceptibly, over time, the fog of detachment began to lift. He realized that something in the game still gave him joy. In the simplicity of the back and forth, in the stroll-rush rhythm, in the short crisp passes, the leaps to head the ball, those arcing long leads and the races for the ball, the shots, the saves and the goals, he once again saw and felt the beauty of the game. It was the game of young men in the joy of their youth. Their exuberance seeped into his pores. He felt a visceral connection to his stolen youth. He found himself cheering, shouting and clapping along with the other fans. At first it was for his team and for the game he was watching. Then, one Sunday afternoon, as he was cheering and shouting, he realized that he was crying. He was crying from the pure joy that came from being released from the horror, death and darkness of which he was still a slave. Soccer, for an afternoon, gave him back the freedom that the camp had taken away.

He became the team's scout at the same time he was promoted to regional buyer for all of stores in Hajdu county. Because his job involved travel, he could recruit players by offering them cushy jobs. That was how Gyuri ended up working at The People's Hardware Store. Sanyi helped to make the team into a contending third-division club. And once Tomi was old enough to walk, Sanyi took him and Gabi to practices and games. And so, Tomi, like his father, became passionate about the game.

6

There is knocking at the front gate.

"Who could it be so early?" His mother looks at his father and instinctively goes to stand by Tomi. He feels her hands squeeze his shoulder.

"Ow." He looks up at her.

She relaxes her grip a little. "Ask who it is before you open the door."

His father is holding a letter. Emma-mama has stopped preparing breakfast. "It's too early for the postman," she says.

"It was Laci."

"Why didn't you invite him in?" Hannah says.

"It was an official visit."

"Why?"

"He was here to deliver a letter."

"For who?" Emma-mama asks. She is afraid of official letters.

"What does it say?" Hannah asks.

October 15, 1956
By order of The Party Commissar Béla Fekete
Of the City of Békes, County of Hajdú
The People's Republic of Hungary

The Department of the Interior summons Wolfstein Sándor, Wolfstein Hannah and Wolfstein Tamás to City Hall in the town of Békes of the County of Hajdú. They are to present themselves without fail Tuesday, 16 October at 8:00 am.

"Why do we have to go to City Hall?" Tomi asks.

"Why do they want Tomi there too?"

"It's probably part of the process before giving us the papers," Sanyi says.

"Why do we have to go to City Hall?" Tomi asks again.

"We asked for permission to travel," his father replies.

"Where are we going?"

"Enough questions. We'll tell you later. Now go get ready for school," his father says.

Tomi didn't like the way his father was acting. He didn't tell jokes anymore, he didn't want to listen to the Sunday soccer games, and he sounded angry when he talked.

"Go. Didn't I tell you to get ready for school?"

He leaves the room but stops outside the door.

"Why do they want us there at eight? City Hall doesn't open until eight thirty," his mother says in a low voice.

"You know what comrade bureaucrats are like. They like to make you wait," Dezsö says.

"I don't like it. Did Laci tell you anything?" Hannah asks.

"No, I'll drop by his office at lunchtime."

———

"So, what did he say?" Hannah wanted to know.

"He said he didn't know anything and he couldn't talk about official business."

"Don't believe him," Dezsö says.

"I tried to find out from others what the decision was but nobody would tell me."

"That's not good." Emma has a worried look.

"I'm sure it'll be okay. I've known Béla since we were young. I always talk to him at soccer games. It has to look like he's following the rules."

"Yes. Rules. No questions. They want to control everything. They don't want you to think for yourself. They want to think for you. That's the problem with the Party."

"Dezsö, don't talk politics around the children!"

"Everything is politics, my dear wife. You know that. The Party controls everything. They make all the decisions and they think they are always right. No wonder people are protesting."

"But because of the Party we have order."

"You know better, Sanyi. It's not order, it's fear."

"And everybody has a job."

"Sure, everybody has a job, but every job is a government job, from street cleaner to soccer player. And every job is controlled by a commissar and if the company commissar doesn't like you, you're fired. And if you don't have a job the government says that you're a hooligan and if you're a hooligan, you're put in jail. So everybody obeys and shuts up. That's the way the party controls you."

Tomi knows that once Dezsö-papa gets started, there is no stopping him.

"It's better than what was before," his father says.

"Is it really?" Dezsö sneers.

"Yes," Emma-mama snaps back. "They can't come after us because we're Jews."

Tomi listens but doesn't really understand what they're talking about.

"The Party takes away people's property and businesses and expects them to work as hard as they did when it was their own. Why should they? They're not crazy. That's why we have shortages."

"But I don't understand why Tomi has to come to City Hall and why we have to be there so early." His mother has that worried tone again.

"People are afraid to speak up or make decisions. If one has to be made, then it's sent up the vertical chain of command like an elevator that stops at every floor."

"And even between."

"Sanyi, don't encourage him."

"It's like those damn matryoshka dolls, dolls inside of dolls. And the dolls are empty and hollow. No wonder the country's a mess."

"Shhh! Not so loud."

"You're always shushing me, woman. That's the problem with this damn country. Everybody is shushing everybody and themselves too. We're a country of shushers! Sanyi, don't be afraid of them. They only have power over you if you remain shushed."

7

"Why do we have to be here?" Tomi asks again as they arrive at City Hall.

"City Hall is a place for grown-ups. It's where grown-ups go for important meetings and important papers," his father says.

"So now I'm a grown-up?"

His father doesn't answer as he pushes down on the brass handle of the thick wooden door that opens into a large empty room. Tomi stops and stares. He feels like he's entering an ogre's cavernous palace like in one of his books about giants. It's dark. He hears jerky steps from inside. He moves closer to his father.

"Let's sit here," his father says quietly, pointing to one of the two long wooden benches that run along either side of the door. He imagines frightened servants on their hands and knees, scrubbing and polishing all night. They sit. Tomi's legs dangle, not quite reaching the floor, which is shiny and slippery. The jerky steps continue but don't seem to be getting closer. He listens and realizes that the sound is coming from the large clock on the wall behind the counter.

The counter, which is taller than he is, looks like it's made of shiny stone with freckles. It stretches from one end of the wall to the other, dividing the room like the picket fence that divides the rose bushes and vegetables from his Golden Green. On it are three shiny gold windows with bars. The room's size and grey walls make him feel that he has to be quiet. There is a poster on each of the walls. All of them are the same; men with rolled-up sleeves and big muscles and women with rosy cheeks, marching, arms raised, holding sickles and hammers, looking up toward a large red sun. The poster is familiar. His classroom has the same picture but with the Little Drummers leading the way. Gabi said he was going to become a Little Drummer next year. Tomi is also anxious to become one because when you become a Little Drummer, you get an Identity Book and get to wear a blue bandana and a special belt with a shiny silver buckle. And you get to practise marching. Maybe that's what it means to be a grown-up.

The posters in this large room look more frightening than friendly. Maybe it's the shadowy darkness. Maybe it's the large shuttered windows that keep the light out. He looks up to see if the lights are on. Soccer ball-sized globes hang from the high ceiling. He hopes that they won't fall on his head. He feels very small.

Two other people enter the room. They look towards Tomi's parents and go to sit on the bench on the other side of the door. It's Mr. and Mrs. Darvas. Tomi knows Mr. Darvas. He is the manager of The People's Butcher Shop and often sits with Tomi's father at soccer games. His father had told Tomi that they'd played soccer together when they were younger. His father nods to them. Mr. Darvas nods back. Mrs. Darvas just stares straight ahead. Everybody sits quietly and waits.

—

Sanyi and Péter Darvas had been bunkmates in labour camp in Szabad. In the early days the conscripts still had a few privileges; once a month they were allowed to receive food and clothing from home. Sanyi never expected anything because his family was too poor. His father had died when he was nine, leaving his mother to manage the best she could. She and his older sister Margit earned a bit of money working from home, tying fringes to prayer shawls. It was only barely enough to survive. Sanyi used to jokingly reminisce that they were so poor that beggars avoided their house because they were afraid that they, the beggars, might be asked to give *them* something.

Péter Darvas was the envy of the bunkhouse. He received monthly packages of food: fried chicken, goose liver or home-made salami. His father was Békes's kosher butcher. Even after the guards, who oversaw the parcel deliveries, took their cut, Péter had plenty. But Péter would never share, not a single bite. One night, after lights out, Sanyi whispered "Péter, share some of that chicken, please."

"No!" Péter barked.

"Which dirty Jew said that?" the bunk sergeant yelled.

Péter was ordered outside and forced to stand at attention, arms in front holding a pickaxe. An hour later, exhausted and in tears, he returned from his punishment, and fell straight into bed. He woke up the next morning to discover that his chicken was gone.

"Sanyi! Did you take my chicken?"

"I saw the pieces just lying there and didn't want the sergeant stealing them. I didn't know how long you would be gone. So I asked myself, what would Péter do in such a case? Would he want it to be eaten by a well-fed gentile sergeant or would he want his starving fellow Jews to help him out in his misfortune? And it was obvious. So, I shared it with the others and told them that it was your gift to them. I did a mitzvah on your behalf."

———

"This is unacceptable. We should not have to be here so early!" Mrs. Darvas tells her husband.

Péter puts his finger to his lips.

"Don't tell me to be quiet!" she hisses. But she says nothing more.

The waiting room is quiet again except for the jerky steps of the clock. Tomi remembers sitting in his father's lap on the steps of the verandah as his father drew a circle in the earth with a stick to teach him how to tell time. His father jabbed the stick in the middle of the circle and showed him, by watching the shadow it cast, what time it was. When Tomi asked him where he learned that neat trick, he said in a place where they had no clocks. Tomi wondered where such a place could be. His father told him that it was secret place he would tell him about when he was older.

Just before eight thirty, a door on the other side of the counter opens and men and women enter in single file. Just like in school. They click-clack across the granite floor. Three of the ladies sit down behind the shiny gold jail windows. He thinks that they look like prisoners, maybe waiting to be rescued. But then he thinks they don't look like they are waiting to be rescued. They look more like they are the guards, looking in on them.

The others disappear from his view. He wonders where they went. The room is as quiet as his classroom before a test. Tomi feels an invisible Mrs. Gombás pacing up and down the aisles.

"Wolfstein Sándor, Wolfstein Hannah, Wolfstein Tamás. Wicket number one." The voice startles him.

They approach the clerk. The lady stamps three pieces of paper really hard. "Here are your numbers. Now sit down and wait," she says, without looking them.

"Thank you." His mother says it so softly that the lady has to look up.

They sit down and his mother looks at the pieces of paper. Each has a number written on it; 01, 02, 03. His father is smiling. Tomi wonders what's funny. Mr. and Mrs. Darvas are called next.

The room is silent again. He's getting tired of sitting. His feet again begin to swing to the jerky sound of the clock. He pretends to be kicking a ball each time the second hand jerks a step forward.

He doesn't like missing school, especially today. Today they're going to practise how to stand properly, how to walk to the front, how to turn to face their classmates, and how to recite their poems clearly and loudly enough so the parents at the back of the room will hear them.

His mother has been helping him every night before bed. She started by reading the poem with him, then just giving him words when he forgot, and later, by mouthing the words with him. The last few days he had even practised with Frog. Each took turns reciting their poems while the other tried to keep the ball in the air without letting it fall to the ground. Even though he can now say it by heart, he doesn't want to miss this last chance to practise with Mrs. Gombás.

"Zero one, zero two, zero three," the lady at wicket number two calls out their numbers. She thrusts her upturned palm at them. "Numbers." She takes the tickets and then stabs them onto a big nail sticking out of the counter. Tomi doesn't like her.

"You will be called. Sit down."

Tomi looks at his parents. They are sitting very straight on the bench, like he does in class, looking ahead and very serious. Since his father's last trip to Budapest, his mother, Emma-mama and even Dezsö-papa seem to be always serious. Maybe being called here was like being called to the principal's office. You had to be very serious. Maybe being a grown-up means that you always had to be serious. But his father and Emma-mama and Dezsö-papa weren't always serious and they were grown-up. Maybe being grown-up means knowing when to be serious. Here he was sure you had to be serious.

—

The hard bench is hurting his behind.

"Be still," his mother whispers, placing her hand on his thigh.

He watches the people behind the granite counter shuffle, sort and stamp papers, move piles of files from desk to desk, stack them on shelves and carry them in and out of offices. He wonders what is behind those large doors. Is it like the principal's office? He has never been in the principal's office. Only kids like Szeles, who got into real trouble, were sent there. Usually, they came back crying. Although his parents told him they were at City Hall to get their travel papers, he senses their tenseness as they stare straight ahead at the busy workers behind the counter.

Finally, wicket lady number three calls them. She asks for their letter and disappears behind a door. Moments later, another lady, looking very serious, opens the centre door and calls out. "Zero one, zero two, zero three. Enter."

The room is dark. A thick black curtain covers the window. A wooden desk and a chair behind it are near the far wall. There are no other chairs. A large soccer-ball-like light hangs from the high ceiling. Pictures of Comrade Marx and Comrade Lenin hang behind the desk. They are also serious. They are the same as those that hang in his class and whose names he and his classmates recite every morning. On either side of the pictures are outlines of rectangles similar to the ones in his classroom after the pictures of Comrade Stalin and Comrade Prime Minister Rákosi were removed.

A door opens from the opposite end of the room and a man in a dark suit enters. It's István's father. He moves forward without looking at them. "Good morning, Mr. Fekete," Tomi says.

István's father looks up, surprised at the greeting. He almost smiles but quickly the stern look returns. He doesn't say anything and quickly sits down. He picks up a folder and slowly opens it. He looks at it for a long time. He puts it down, takes a cigarette from his pack, lights it, looks up at them sternly. Then looks down at the folder again. Tomi is scared. Mr. Fekete was always friendly to him when he went over to István's house. He sometimes even gave them money to buy rock candy. Tomi looks at his parents, who are standing still, like statues. After Mr. Fekete takes a few drags of his cigarette, he looks up again.

"So, comrades, you have applied to leave the Motherland?"

"Feri," his father began.

"I am Comrade Commissar Fekete and you will address me so."

Tomi looks up at his father. His father looks very serious. He looks Mr. Fekete in the eyes and nods. "Comrade Commissar Fekete. With all due respect, the government has allowed people who want to emigrate to Israel to do so."

"No! The government has allowed Jews *to apply* for an exit visa."

"That is true. I stand corrected."

"Therefore, the question is, what true Hungarian would want to apply?" the Commissar asked.

"We are true Hungarians, Comrade Commissar," Tomi's mother says. "We were born here. Our son was born here. My father served in the army in the First World War."

"Is he still alive?" he asks.

"Yes, God keep him."

"And after he did his patriotic duty for you and the Motherland, you now want to abandon your father and country?"

His parents say nothing.

"These are heroic times, comrades," Mr. Fekete begins in a softer tone. "Hungary needs her people to defend her. Great changes are coming. We need every man, woman and child to help Hungary in her time of need. True Hungarians must stand together shoulder to shoulder to defend each other and their Motherland."

Tomi feels his father's grip tighten on his hand. It hurts but he bites his lip and stares ahead.

"Comrade Commissar Fekete, with all due respect, please tell me where were my fellow Hungarians when my fellow Hungarians in Black Shirts patrolled Békes, forbidding me to walk the streets of my town? Where were my comrades when the Guardians of Silence and the Gestapo came to take my mother to Auschwitz? Who stood shoulder to shoulder to defend us? Feri, when we were young, you and I played soccer together as our children do now. Where were you, Comrade Commissar, when I needed my true Hungarian heroes to stand shoulder to shoulder with me?"

Tomi doesn't know what his father is talking about. Why was his family taken away? What is this Auschwitz he is now hearing about for the second time? Why is his father so angry at István's father?

Mr. Fekete gets up quickly. Tomi takes a step back. His father pulls him back. István's father walks around from his desk and waves the documents at them. "Refused!" he shouts, throwing the papers at them. Tomi watches the papers float through the air, slowly, like autumn leaves, until they lie scattered on the floor. For a moment, no one moves. Then his father reaches down and picks Tomi up. He feels like he is flying straight up. His father and mother turn toward the door. Looking over his father's shoulder, Tomi watches István's father down on one knee, gathering the papers.

8

The crackling on the other side of the wall keeps Tomi awake. It sounds like the crumpling of paper. Tomi listens to make out what is going on. Voices fade in and out.

"They're jamming the radio again."

"...Radio Free America..."

"...Hungarian freedom..."

"...courageous..."

"...with you."

"Sanyi, turn it down. The boys are asleep."

"Sounds like the Americans aren't going to come."

" ...demand they leave...or..."

"The Russians aren't going to leave."

"They already have. I heard it."

"This is not good for us."

"It's not good for the Communists." Dezsö-papa sounds glad. "But the Russians aren't going to let it happen."

"There's been nothing on the radio about it."

"We have to go. We must."

"I'm not trying it again. I'm not going to prison again. Once was enough. They're not going to take Gabi away from me a second time."

"I hate them all, but Emma's right."

More crumpling sounds come from the radio. "I think that's it for tonight," his father says.

When was Emma-mama in prison? And why? He had never heard of a lady going to jail. He can't imagine her locked up in one of those dark cells he had seen in the adventure books his mother read to him. Not Emma. She's such a good person. Tomi hears footsteps and squeezes his eyes shut, pretending to be asleep as his parents prepare for bed.

"I vowed to Faigele and my mother's memory, *never again*. I won't let it happen again," he hears his mother whisper to his father. "I meant it."

Tomi falls asleep wondering what his mother won't let happen again.

—

Tomi is in a forest. The forest is very dark. He's being chased. He doesn't know what is chasing him, but he knows it's gaining on him. He's running but not moving. The air has a smoky smell. A strong wind is blowing against him. The leaves are slapping him in the face. His lungs are on fire. A big rough hand reaches down from the sky. It's pressing on his head, pushing him down into sucking mud. He tries to push it off. It's too strong. The palm pushes harder. With a loud sucking sound, the earth swallows him up. He's in a tunnel. There's a smell of earthy rotten roots. The tunnel is small. He's on all fours. He can't stand. He freezes. There's thumping above him. Each thump is followed by a growling-rumble. There are side tunnels going off in different directions. He starts to crawl, but each one leads him back to where he started. The roots are reaching for him. The earth above him gives way. He looks up. Dirt starts to rain on him. It falls in his eyes, nose, ears and mouth. He's choking. He can't breathe. He looks up. A large boot is coming down on him. Its toe opens like a mouth. It has glistening spiky teeth. Tomi screams.

"I can't see! I can't see!"

He feels the teeth bite into his wrists. It starts to yank and shake him. He tries to free his arms but the teeth just hold on tighter and tighter.

"Tomi! Tomi! Wake up! It's okay. You're just having a bad dream."

The morning is chilly and clear. The sun reflects brightly off his polished chrome-plated handlebars. He and Gabi take the roundabout route, pedalling along rutted wagon tracks and cow paths, through the flat muddy commons, past Mishka, the town herder, who yells at them as the geese scatter, past the well where the Gypsy girls gather to draw water, through a thicket of leafless trees, ducking the stinging whips of branches. He imagines himself a Hajdú on his noble steed, galloping into a glorious battle against the terrible Turks. He lowers his head and pedals faster.

They arrive at school grinning and breathless. They jump off their bikes like Hajdús off their steeds and park them next to the others. Their Superla bikes outshine the others.

They run to take their places just as the first whistle for line-up sounds. The bell rings and everybody marches inside.

Tomi likes the poem he's memorized because it's about a boy who doesn't want to go to sleep, even though his mother tells him about all the things that have already gone to sleep and urges him to do the same. He likes it because he doesn't like going to sleep either. Especially while the adults stay up. He knows that nighttime is the time for secrets and adventures. He's sure that while he's asleep, he's missing out on something exciting. Especially lately. Ever since the visit to City Hall, the parents are staying up later and speaking in voices more hushed than usual.

He also doesn't like the adventures he's been having in his dreams.

Today is the last day before the recital. Mrs. Gombás is going to call on each student to recite. Tomi closes his eyes and concentrates on his poem. He hears Mrs. Gombás reminding them not to forget the title and the poet's name. He practised and practised. He knows it by heart.

Lullaby by Josef Attila

The sky shuts its blue–blue eyes
The houses too, shut their many eyes
Under eiderdown sleep the fields
So you too, sleep sweetly, my darling young son.

Upon their folded legs, sleep
The insects and the wasps
And with them sleep their hums
So you too, sleep sweetly, my darling young son.

The streetcar is sleeping too
And slumbers too its rumblings
In his dream his bell jingles once —
So you too, sleep sweetly, my darling young son.

Upon the chair sleeps the coat
Dozing too its tear
No more will it rip today
So you too, sleep sweetly, my darling young son.

Sleeps the ball and whistle
The woods and the picnics as well
The good candy is sleeping too —
So you too, sleep sweetly, my darling young son.

The far-off distance, like the agate
Marble you will have; a giant
you will be, if you just close your eyes —
So sleep sweetly, my darling young son.

A fireman, a soldier you will be
A shepherd of wild beasts
See, your mama is nodding off
So you too, sleep sweetly, my darling young son.

"Tamás Wolfstein."

Tomi's eyes snap open. He stands at attention.

"Come to the front."

Tomi walks slowly from the back of the room. He smiles at his teacher. He knows that he is her favourite. But she isn't smiling today. She has on her serious face, the one she wears when the class isn't progressing. Maybe she is angry because of all the problems the other kids are having reciting. Maybe she is worried that they won't be able to do it well enough for the principal and the parents. He is determined to do it flawlessly. He wants her to be proud of him. He wants to be perfect, for her.

When he turns to face the class, he feels Mrs. Gombás's hand on his head. She turns him firmly toward her. Her face looks hard, her lips are tight and her eyes make him feel cold.

"So, Hungary is not your homeland? So, you want to leave your Motherland and go to your Jewland?"

He feels as though a thousand bees have stung him. His cheeks feel like they're on fire. He wants to cry but doesn't want his classmates to see him. He clenches his jaws and fists. Mrs. Gombás gasps, grabs him by the shoulder and turns him to face the class.

"Take a good look. This is what a traitor looks like. This class is only for true Hungarians. Now leave at once, you dirty little Jew."

"I won't cry. I won't cry," he tells himself silently over and over again as he marches out of class and down the empty, silent corridor that seems to go on forever. The only sound comes from the metal taps of his shoes clacking against the floor.

He doesn't understand. Teachers only punish you when you do something wrong. What did he do wrong? It isn't his fault that he's a Jew. He isn't a traitor. He wants to play soccer for the Hungarian national team.

The noon bell rings.

Szeles and three of his gang are standing around the bike rack, smiling. Tomi eyes each of them. And then he sees his bike.

Its tires are flat. Some of the bright red enamel has been scraped away, the chain is off and coated with dirt and his Superla logo is missing!

"You stupid animal!" he screams and charges, taking Szeles by surprise. They fall to the ground. Tomi fights to stay on top. He hits Szeles as hard as he can. Blood spurts from Szeles' nose as Tomi hits him repeatedly. He is hitting Mrs. Gombás. He is hitting István's father. He is hitting the boot with the spiky teeth.

"I won't cry. I won't cry!" he shouts.

Szeles throws him off and rolls over onto him, pinning Tomi's arms with his legs. Szeles's blood drips onto Tomi's face as Szeles hits him and spits on him.

"Jews! Jews! Dirty Jews eat dirt!" he shouts. He grabs a handful of dirt to stuff down Tomi's throat. Tomi tries to twist away but Szeles grabs him by the hair and smears dirt all over his face. "Jews eat dirt."

Suddenly Szeles is off him. He sees Gabi on top of Szeles. Szeles's friends grab Gabi, but Carrot, Frog and István grab them. They are all grabbing and tugging at each other. Tomi scrambles up, reaches into his pocket and pulls out his knife. The blade springs out. "You stupid animal," he screams. Everyone freezes. Tomi charges. He rams the blade of his knife to the hilt into the front tire of Szeles's bike. Szeles grabs Tomi by his shirt collar and yanks. The knife flies out of his hands as he is thrown back down onto the ground. Gabi grabs Szeles and spins him off Tomi.

A crowd gathers around the boys. "Hit him! Kick him! Punch him in the head! Yes! Yes!" they shout.

"Stop it! Stop it!" It's Mr. Toth. He breaks through the circle, his slashing pointer hitting everyone within reach.

"Stop it! Stop it!" he shouts as he continues to swing the pointer left and right, forcing the crowd of boys back. "Stand up! All of you!" Then he turns to the crowd that has gathered. "Leave! Now! Everybody!"

No one moves. "Now!" Mr. Toth shouts, raising the pointer high overhead. Reluctantly, the mob of boys backs off and disperses.

Mr. Toth faces the boys. "Stand up straight! Animals. You're all animals! Hooligans! What kind of behaviour is this?"

"That Jew tried to stab me with his knife."

Mr. Toth turned his gaze accusingly on Tomi. "Did you do that?"

"No. I attacked his bike because but he did it to mine first."

"No, I didn't!"

"Enough. I don't want to hear another word from any of you hooligans. You are all to be at the principal's office at eight thirty sharp tomorrow morning. With your parents! Do you understand?"

No one speaks.

"I didn't hear you. Are you all deaf and dumb?"

"Yes, Sir!" everyone replies at once.

"Now leave!" he snaps.

Szeles and his friends grab their bikes and run down the lane. Just before he turns the corner, Szeles sticks out his arm holding the Superla ornament in his hand and yells, "Heil Hitler." Mr. Toth spins around, but by then Szeles and his gang have disappeared. Looking at Tomi and Gabi, he sighs. "Be careful, boys," he says quietly. Then he turns and, with his head down, walks back toward the school.

Tomi and Gabi wheel their bikes out of the schoolyard, their friends trailing close behind.

"What happened?" Gabi asks.

"Stupid Mrs. Gombás," Frog says.

"What happened?"

"She called Tomi a dirty little Jew."

"Why? What did you do?" Gabi asked.

"Nothing!"

"It was his turn to recite his poem and she just started calling him a traitor and a dirty little Jew."

"He's a dirty little Jew now," Carrot says, looking at him.

"So is Frog," István says, looking at Frog.

"No, I'm not. I'm a dirty *Gypsy*," Frog says, spitting out bits of dust. "Here," he says, and hands Tomi his knife.

9

Instead of going straight home with Gabi, Tomi walks his bike toward his father's store, the way a wounded Hajdú might lead his weary steed after a battle. He keeps his eyes down so he won't be recognized and won't have to look at anyone. The store, on the north side of the square, faces the Heroic Russian Soldier statue. He stops in front of the store window, trying to decide what to do next. Before his father was made to work in the basement, Tomi used to just run in whenever he wanted to see him. But now everything is different. He hesitates. He decides to wait outside.

He puts his bike on its kick stand. The outline of where the Superla logo used to be stares at him. He strokes the crossbar. The scratched paint rasps against his fingers. The chain, caked with dirt, hangs loosely around the front chain ring. He kneels and slowly turns the front tire. It has three slashes. He squats down next to his bike with his back to the store window.

The day has been a disaster. He wasn't allowed to recite the poem that he has practised so often. He was expelled from class because he was a traitor and a Jew. He was in a fight. His nice school clothes are covered with blood and dirt, and his bike is a wreck. And he has to tell his parents that they have to go to the principal's office. He's never been in so much trouble. His puffy cheeks throb. The skin around his eyes is tender to the touch. It hurts, but in a way, it feels good.

The sound of singing makes him look up. He can't see clearly. The swelling has almost shut his eye and the tearing makes it difficult to see. He can make out blobs that he knows are people marching towards him. They seem to be shimmering. As they get closer and louder he can make out men carrying ropes, a ladder, pickaxes, sledgehammers, staves and sickles. They're singing the national anthem. He can see people leaning out of windows and coming out of buildings and standing in doorways to see what's going on.

The crowd comes to a halt in the square. They stop singing. Their leader stands beneath the statue and begins to recite. Many join in.

Rise, O Magyar! 'Tis your country's call:
Now is the time, say one and all:
Shall we be slaves, shall we be free?
This is the question, choose to be!
By the Magyar's God, we truly swear,
The tyrant's yoke no more to bear!

He recognizes the words. It's the poem he heard with his mother on the first day of school. His class has started to learn it. Mrs. Gombás told them that the great poet Petöfi Sándor wrote it and it inspired the brave Hungarians in the 1848 revolution against the Austrians and that it had become Hungary's national poem. And Petöfi recited it before he rode off into battle, where he died fighting bravely for the noble cause of Hungarian freedom.

He remembers his mother saying that "it wasn't for them," but until this morning, until Mrs. Gombás told him that he was a traitor, he felt that the poem was about him and his country, and he recited it with pride.

When they finish, the leader begins climbing the ladder that had been placed against the statue, while a couple of other men hold it secure. The man on the ladder places three nooses around the Heroic Russian Soldier's neck and tosses down the ropes to the waiting men.

Once down he points to the statue and, as a captain before leading his men into battle, shouts, "Now, Hungarian patriots, for the freedom of the Motherland, pull!" They pull and grunt and pull, but the statue won't budge.

Others run up to help. They too pull and grunt and pull, but still the soldier won't move. More people joined them.

"One, two, three—pull!" the leader calls. "One, two, three, pull!" The soldier starts to lean, at first just enough to look like he is bending over to see who is bothering him. But slowly he reaches the tipping point. Everyone stands still. Waiting. It's like a poster in which heroic socialist men are pulling together. Tomi holds his breath. It feels like forever. And then, as if the statue has given up the fight, it comes crashing down face first. People scramble out of the way. With a loud thump, it lands in the gravel. There is a sharp crack. The neck snaps, breaks off and rolls away from the body. The crowd bursts into a cheer, the kind Tomi has often heard on the radio after a Puskás goal.

People with sledgehammers and pickaxes start pounding away at the headless soldier. "Freedom! Freedom!" they chant.

"Oh, my God! Tomi! What happened? What happened?" He hadn't seen his father come out of the store. His father lifts him into his arms. By now one of Tomi's eyes has swollen almost closed. His father is shouting to be heard above the yelling of the crowd. "What in God's good name has happened to you?"

Suddenly there is an explosion. Somebody screams, "The Russians are coming! The Russians are coming!" Everybody starts to scream, "The Russians are coming!" All at once, like frightened geese, the crowd scatters in every direction.

"My bicycle!" Tomi cries, as his father runs with him in his arms. But his father doesn't hear. He is just running, holding him tight. When Tomi turns to look over his father's shoulder, he sees his bicycle now part of the litter of picks, axes and ropes in the abandoned square and in the flowerbed, the head of the heroic Russian soldier staring up at the cloudless sky.

"Rotten lice! Rotten lice!" His mother repeats over and over again as she applies a cold compress to his swollen eye. "The one place in this louse-ridden dirty world I thought he would be safe!" she hisses. "I should know better by now."

"Tomi winces at the pressure. "I want my bicycle back!"

"We'll get it tomorrow." His father strokes his head. "I promise."

"The Russians didn't come," Dezsö-papa says. "I was just talking with Jóska. It was a truck that backfired. It doesn't take much to frighten those patriots."

"May they all be infested with lice and their children and their children's children!" his mother curses. He has never heard his mother angry like this.

"Emma, close and shutter the windows."

"Come on, Dezsö," his father says. The two men go out.

A few minutes later Tomi hears a loud clang echo in the house. It sounds like a castle gate being barred or maybe a jail door closing.

"Let those animals try to get through that!" Gabi's father strides back in, spits into his palms and slaps his palms together a couple of times.

"Hold this on your eye for a few more minutes," his mother says. Tomi, holding the cold compress, goes out, sits next to Gabi and watches him clean his bike's chain.

"Gabi, why do people hate the Jews?"

"Because we killed Jesus Christ."

"Who's Jesus Christ?"

"He's God's son. Carrot said that the Jews killed him and that's why everyone hates us."

"When did we kill him?"

"I don't know, a long time ago."

"Why?"

Gabi shrugs his shoulders. "I don't know."

"What did Carrot say?

"He didn't know either."

"How can you kill God's son?"

"You hammer nails in his hands and feet and put him on a cross."

"That must hurt. More than a whack from Mr. Toth."

"Supper!" Emma-mama calls.

Gabi's father is trying to get a clear reception. "It's not too bad. Let's hear what the liars from the outside world are saying."

Everyone gathers around the table while Gabi's mother spoons stew into their bowls.

"…left…Moscow agreed to withdraw…brave Hungarians fight on…we are with you."

"The Americans aren't coming." His mother talks to the radio.

"And the Russians aren't leaving," says Dezsö-papa, taking a shot of pálinka.

"But the radio's been saying for days that they're leaving."

"Sanyi, you can't believe those Americans," Dezsö-papa says and pours himself another shot.

"Why not? They liberated us. Didn't they?"

"Yes, but that was different."

"You met Americans?" Tomi asked his father, his one good eye widening.

"Yes."

"Did you meet cowboys?" Gabi asked.

"No."

"Indians?" Tomi asked.

"No." His father was smiling. He hasn't seen his father smile in a long time.

"Were you in jail?"

"No. Prison camp."

"Were you prisoners during the war?" Gabi asked.

"Slaves." Gabi's father says.

The reception is getting bad again. Tomi's father turns off the radio.

"You were slaves? Tell us more." It sounds exciting to Tomi.

"It's time for you boys to get ready for bed," Emma-mama says.

"Please," Tomi and Gabi plead.

"It's not for bedtime stories. It will give you bad dreams. Another time," his father tells him.

"To bed now," Emma-mama says again, pushing them firmly out of the kitchen.

Tomi wonders what Americans look like, if they all wear cowboy hats, if they ride horses, if they shoot Indians. And why was his father a slave? Did he have to wear chains? Weren't slaves from long time ago? He just found out that Emma-mama and Dezsö-papa had been in prison and now he finds out that his father was a slave. Maybe his mother also? What crimes did they commit? Only bad people who did bad things were put in prison. Maybe Mrs. Gombás called him a traitor because his parents had been slaves and killed Jesus Christ. He hears his parents talking out on the verandah. He opens the door quietly and sees them standing, looking into the yard.

"It's getting dark earlier and earlier."

"And chillier. Winter's coming. Sanyi, we have to go."

His father puts his arms around his mother. Tomi has never seen him do this before. "We'll be all right."

"I want to kill them."

"Let's go back inside, Hannah."

Tomi wonders if his parents were killers before he was born.

—

"I'm not going to go to see the principal and Tomi is not going back until all this is over," his mother says. Tomi wants to go even though he knows that Mrs. Gombás doesn't want him in her class. Emma-mama tries to keep them busy. She has them turn the soil and prepare the vegetable garden for winter, practise their addition and subtraction, and quiz each other on the capitals of countries. She has them read *The Count of Monte Cristo*, her favourite, out loud. Tomi draws pictures in his notebook of Puskás kicking the ball while Gabi draws Grosics leaping, making saves. The days are getting cold, but not enough to stop them from kicking the ball around in the yard. When it's too cold or raining, they go help the blacksmiths and play with Attila.

The radio is always on. Radio Petöfi, the same station that broadcasts the Honvéd games, now plays music that isn't only Hungarian or Russian. Emma-mama says it's American. It sounds faster and louder. Between songs, there is constant talk about things he doesn't understand.

The talk at suppertime is always serious.

"They're not revolutionaries, just hooligans and fascists," his mother says when the radio urges Hungarians to fight.

"What are fascists? Tomi asks.

"They're hooligans in pressed shirts," Gabi's father says.

"We must have socialist justice. There must be an end to corruption and the AVO must be disbanded," the man on the radio says. Music starts to play.

"What's AVO?" Gabi asks.

"It's a special police," Tomi's father says.

"Vicious animals," Dezsö-Papa spits. "They were the ones who arrested us and put us in jail."

This is the second time Tomi has heard about Gabi's parents being in jail.

"Were you bad?" he asks

"No," Emma-mama answers.

"Then why?"

A deep, serious voice interrupts the music. "We bring you a special bulletin."

"Listen," Tomi's father says. Everyone stops talking. "Puskás and other members of Budapest Honvéd soccer team have defected!"

The minute he hears Puskás's name Tomi stops eating. "What happened? What's defected?"

His father waves a hand to silence him.

"What happened?" Tomi asks again.

"Shh!" his father hisses, staring at the radio.

"Puskás, as captain, speaks on the team's behalf."

"We, in solidarity with the brave patriots of Hungary, have decided to stop our Western European tour. We will not play any more games while the Soviet Army is occupying our country. And we will not return until they leave."

"What's defected?"

"It means that the team has decided not to be Communist anymore. They're brave now that they're out of the country," Dezsö-papa says.

"Why don't they want to be Communists anymore?"

"They want the Russians to go home," his father answers.

"I don't want the Russians to go. They're good for us," his mother says.

"But if they stay, Puskás and the team won't come home."

"That's not our problem," she says.

"The great Hungarian revolution is succeeding. We urge resistance," the announcer declares. "And now we return to our regular musical programming and to our patriot Ida Boros singing 'Homesickness.'"

"Turn it off," his mother says. "I've had enough of this stupidity."

"Oh, I love this song," Emma-mama says. "I want to hear it."

"What homesickness? What a homeland!" his mother says as she leaves the kitchen.

He sits on his perch on the verandah watching his Golden-Green disappear in the early evening darkness. So much is happening so fast. Not only has he stopped going to school, he has even stopped attending Chaider. Not that he misses it, but still, it would be better than staying home all the time. Frog and Carrot still come by, but he wants to be playing on the school field. Even breakfast with the blacksmiths has become quieter.

What happened, Tomi wonders, to turn Békes from a friendly place into a mean one? Why does everyone look so serious, so grown-up? And now Puskás, his hero, doesn't want to come home! Are he and the team traitors also?

Usually, at supper there is a lot of talking. But lately it's been getting quieter. Tonight it is almost silent. His father and mother are looking at each other and at Emma-mama and Dezsö-papa in a very serious way. Something is wrong, but he doesn't know what it is and is afraid to ask. After supper Emma-mama lights the storm lantern, turns it down so low that the wick barely shows and puts it on the kitchen table. His mother turns off the lights. Except for the pale glow of the storm lantern, the house is dark.

He has gotten used to Emma-mama shuttering the windows and closing the curtains and his father and Dezsö-papa barring the door, but this is the first time they have turned off the light so early in the evening.

Tomi and Gabi, in identical flannel pyjamas that Tomi's mother made for them from material sent by Margit, snuggle in their mothers' laps. He feels like his mother is holding him tighter than usual. He tries to wiggle loose. She pulls him closer.

Dezsö-papa brings out a bottle of pálinka and pours each of the grown-ups a shot. "Let them try to come in," he says, downing his glass in one gulp. Tomi's father throws back his drink too and lets out a quick breath.

"Who?" Tomi asks.

His father leans over and gently kisses the top of his head. He can smell his father's warm fruity breath.

"Don't worry. Nothing bad will happen," he says. "Maybe some drunk hooligans will try to break in, but they won't be able to."

Tomi sees his father pick up a hammer and sit by the door. Gabi's father, sickle in hand, joins him. Emma-mama has her broom at her side, while his mother's kitchen knife is in front of her on the table. He looks at Gabi. They jump off their mothers' laps and run to the ceramic stove. They reach behind it and draw out the swords the blacksmiths made for them. Standing at attention on either side of the stove, Tomi imagines himself and Gabi to be like Hajdús ready for battle.

"Oh my God." Emma-mama starts to weep.

"Where did you get those daggers?" Tomi's mother asks.

Last year, the blacksmiths told Tomi that they would make them swords if their parents allowed. Tomi asked and his mother was adamantly against it, but Tomi told the blacksmiths at the beginning of the school year that his parents had agreed. It was their secret. They'd go into the woods beside the soccer field next to the cemetery and slash at branches, pretending they were the Turks. Sometimes they fought each other, the click-clack of steel on steel making them feel brave. Sometimes, by accident, they nicked each other. When they did, they sucked the blood, spat it out heroically and looked on their cuts as bravely earned wounds.

"They're swords," Tomi says. Though he is expecting his mother to chastise him for lying, he sees that his mother is more sad than angry.

"Jóska made them," Gabi adds. "And they have dragons on them."

"Maybe it's time to tell them about the war. They should know," Tomi's mother says.

"What?" Tomi asks.

"No," his father says. "This is not the time."

"If not now, then when?"

"I learned about the war."

Dezsö waved his hand to quiet them. "Listen!"

At first they don't hear anything. Then a whisper of sounds like the hiss of steam when Jóska dips a red-hot iron into the bucket of cold water. Then the clip-clop of boots on cobblestone. The whisper rises to a chant. "Death to Communists! Death to Jews!"

Tomi doesn't want to be scared but he is. He runs and stands next to his father. He doesn't understand. He knows what a Communist is. He learned that it was good to be a Communist. It's written in his books and on posters everywhere. Mrs. Gombás taught them that Communism made everyone equal. Communist comrades build socialism together. All Hungarians were good Communists. So he doesn't understand why they now wanted to kill themselves. And the Jews.

He is a Jew. But he is pretty sure that his family didn't kill Jesus Christ a long time ago. He thought a lot about it after Gabi told him that the Jews killed Jesus Christ. He can imagine Gabi's father arguing with Jesus, but not killing him. And he can't imagine Rabbi Stern or Yossie killing Jesus either.

"Death to Communists! Death to Jews!"

As the chanting grows louder, Tomi begins to understand something that he'd never thought about before these last few weeks. He is different. And because he's different he's not wanted. Mrs Gombás, Szeles and the others don't want him to be one of them. Mrs. Gombás called him a traitor. His mother was right.

The marching stops, but the chanting continues in front of their house. His father peeks through the shutters.

"There are about thirty of them."

"Oh my God!" Emma-mama cries out.

Dezsö-papa shushes her. Tomi's mother orders the boys to stand near the closet. "If you hear them coming in, go hide in there and stay there until we come for you."

"I'm not afraid," Gabi says

"Just do what I say. You understand?"

He nods.

"Gabi, you're the older one, so you have to take care of Tomi."

"Yes."

"I can fight."

"Take care of each other!" his mother says.

"This is Sándor Wolfstein's house," a man yells out. Tomi recognizes the voice. He hears it daily. He can't believe the man wants to hurt them.

"It's Jóska," Sanyi whispers. Everyone runs to the window.

There they are, Jóska, Zoli and Fire, hammers resting on their shoulders. They stand facing the crowd.

"This is Sándor Wolfstein's house," Jóska repeats. "And no one is going in. No one is going to touch them. Or he will have to deal with us."

Attila barks.

Tomi looks through the slats. Under the streetlamp, Jóska, Zoli and Fire look like powerful giants standing guard at a castle gate. For a moment, there is silence. It's as if everyone is a statue. Only their breaths move, rising like dragons' smoke made visible by the streetlamp.

"Jew lover!" someone yells. Attila barks again. There is silence.

"We'll remember this, Jóska," yells another.

"Good," Jóska shouts back.

There is silence. Tomi listens.

"Come on, boys. Let's visit that stinking rabbi." There is a loud cheer and the mob turns and disappears into the same darkness from which it came.

———

"Hannah, please don't go. Not alone," Emma pleads.

"I'm just going out for some vegetables, and then to meet Sanyi. They don't have the courage to do anything during the day."

"Can I go with you?" Tomi asks.

"No," she says, bending over and kissing him. She puts on her coat, picks up the basket and slips the paring knife into her pocket. Emma-mama clasps her hand as if in prayer. "Be careful. Be careful."

Hannah walks toward the market, her wicker basket in one hand and in the other, in her pocket, the paring knife. People who normally stopped to talk, or at least nod, hurry by.

You insects think that if you avoid me you can tell yourselves that nothing is wrong, Hannah says to herself. But I've smelled this rot of hate before. You want to act as if nothing happened, to go on as if things are normal. But I know you rotten lice. Only at night do you crawl out and show your true face. I swore the last time I'd never forget what you did to my family, and I swear now

I won't forget you pack of animals, desecrating the cemetery and the synagogue, beating and stuffing the rabbi into the chicken coop. And I swear I won't forget what you've done to my son. I swear, I won't ever forget and I'll never forgive.

She spits on the sidewalk and tightens her grip on the knife.

At the market, she makes sure to look the merchants in the eyes. And when they hold out their hands for payment, she stares until they lower theirs.

She continues toward the station. On Saturday evenings in summertime, the Wolfsteins were one of the many families that would promenade up and down Market Street, basking in the evening warmth. After the war, a quiet amble along the elm-lined street felt like a great event. For Hannah the fact that they could stroll to the train station and back at their leisure was special. And stopping on the way home at the ice cream parlour for an ice cream made the return walk sweet. Watching Tomi's eyes light up when Sanyi handed him his cone of cherry ice cream, watching him bite into that solid mouth-freezing red scoop and gasp each time with the joy and innocence only a child experiences, that was sweet and special.

But now, as she walks past the ice cream parlour, a taste of what's happening in Békes rises in her mouth, so sour a thousand ice creams wouldn't get rid of it.

10

"It's arranged. We're leaving tonight," Tomi's father announces to everyone the minute he walks through the door. "The seven o'clock train."

"Tonight?" Emma-mama asks. She has a frightened look.

"Leaving? Where are we going?" Tomi asks.

"We're going to Sopron for a little while," his mother says.

"Why Sopron? I thought we wanted to go to Israel." His parents exchange a look, then his father says, "You're a big boy now, so I will tell you. We're going to Sopron and from there we will go to Israel. We're leaving tonight, but it's a secret, so you can't tell anyone. Do you understand?"

"Can I tell Frog?"

"No."

"You can send him a nice postcard when we get there. It will be a special surprise for him."

"How long are we going for?"

"If we're lucky, for a long time."

"Is Gabi coming?"

"No…"

"Yes. We're going too," Dezső-papa says.

"What are you saying?" Emma-mama cries out.

"I thought you didn't want to take the chance again," Hannah says.

Sanyi is taken aback. "Are you sure? Even after last time?"

"Sanyi, what's the point of staying in this pigsty?"

"Dezső…"

"Emma, why do we want to stay in a place where we have to always worry about hooligans trying to beat down our door? Worry about Gabi all the time? Sleep with one eye open and one ear cocked? We won't have the blacksmiths standing guard for the rest of our lives. I'm ready to try again."

Tomi's mother embraces Emma-mama.

"Go outside and play a while," Tomi's father says. It is crisp with a slight wind but snow hasn't fallen yet. The ground hasn't frozen but it's hard. They kick the ball back and forth.

"Gabi, where's Sopron?"

"In fifth place."

"I mean in the country."

"Oh. Near Austria, I think."

"Where is Israel?"

"Somewhere in the desert."

"Papa told me when we were coming back from City Hall that it was a country filled with Jews, a country where nobody hates us."

"Imagine," Gabi said. "A country full of Rabbi Sterns."

Tomi laughs and kicks the ball high into the blacksmiths' yard.

"Hey, Puskás," Fire calls to Tomi as he rolls the ball back to him. "What's up?"

"We're going—" Tomi begins, but remembering his father's warning, snaps his mouth shut.

"You're going where?"

"Nowhere." Tomi answers, taking back the ball.

Walking back to his side of the fence, he stops and looks around. It is beginning to get dark. With the flowers and leaves gone, the rose bushes look like the tangled prickly witch's hair in his old Hansel and Gretel book. The vegetable garden, which in summer was rows of lush greens and reds, is now just a rectangle of dried earth, rows of little graves, with only a few scraggly shoots showing. And his Golden Green looks like a sad and abandoned field. He doesn't want to go away. And even though bad things have happened to him and his family in Békes, he likes it here. His best friend Frog is here, and the blacksmiths are here. And everything.

—

"I want to take my soccer ball. And my soccer sweater. And my sword. And my book." His mother has read *The Paul Street Boys* to him twice already, but now he is reading it on his own. He is at the part where Nemecsek, the smallest and weakest of the Paul Street boys, has been made fun of because of his smallness and weakness by his own gang. To prove them wrong he spies on the Redshirts and is captured. They interrogate him about the fortifications by dunking him in the icy lake, but he does not betray his pals.

"That's too much," his mother says.

"But I need my soccer ball."

"No."

"Please!"

"No."

He begins to sniffle. "Please!"

"Don't do that. Big boys don't cry," his mother snaps.

"We can deflate it and stuff it in with the sweater," his father suggests.

"All right." She sighs. "But nothing else."

Tomi runs to the ceramic fireplace and takes his sword from behind.

"No!" his mother says firmly.

"I'm just going to hide it so I'll have it when I come back."

He looks around for a good hiding place.

"How about under the bed?" she says.

"No."

"Under the sofa?"

"No."

"In the armoire?"

"No. Anybody could find it in those places. Too easy. I don't want anyone else to have my sword."

He holds it aloft, as if ready to charge. He runs to the kitchen, finds Emma-mama's ball of twine and takes off out the door, twine in one hand, sword in the other. "Don't run with it," his mother yells after him. He pretends he doesn't hear her and runs to the well. He ties one end of the twine around the hilt of the sword and makes a loop at the other. He leans over the lip of the well and lowers the sword, trying to attach it to a hook in the wall of the well below the water line from which his parents hang bottles of milk to keep cool. Tomi's father watches from the verandah.

"Don't lean over too far," his father calls.

"Help me. I can't reach it."

His father joins him at the well, and Tomi hands him the sword.

"No," his father says, "you do it."

His father lifts him up and holds him as he leans over the edge of the well. Tomi sees their reflection looking back at them. For a moment both just stare. Slowly, Tomi lowers the sword into the well and slips the loop onto the hook. Their reflections break into ripples and the sword disappears into the dark water.

Gabi has come out of the house with his sword. "I want to put mine there too."

"Go ahead." Tomi's father hands Gabi the ball of twine.

Gabi is tall enough to do it himself. He leans over, hooks the twine on and slowly lowers his sword.

"It's a good hiding place, isn't it?"

"Excellent," Tomi's father says.

Tomi and Gabi hold hands and walk back to the house.

"What about my bicycle?"

"Your Aunt Magda will come and take care of it."

His mother looks around. "We worked so hard for all of this. Rotten lice."

"We'll have better, I promise."

Tomi sticks the air pin into the hole and sits on his soccer ball to push out all the air. As he sits on the hissing, deflating ball he watches his mother stuffs socks, underwear and one of his shirts into his father's briefcase. She folds one of her blouses into a smaller and smaller square, until it's small enough to slip into her handbag, along with two pairs of nylons that she strokes a couple of times before putting them in.

"It has to look like we're just taking an after-supper walk," his father said.

"I baked some pogácsa yesterday. We can take them," Emma-mama says, as they all gather in the kitchen.

Tomi loves Emma-mama's pogácsa. When they are fresh from the oven, he loves peeling off the upper crisp, golden layer, inhaling the rising steam from the buttery dough. And whenever Emma-mama packs a few of them into his schoolbag, he imagines himself as a hero setting off on an adventure just like the heroes in his folktale books.

"I'm going to miss those chickens. They're no lazy communists. They're good layers," Gabi's father says. Emma-mama hard-boils the eggs. Along with a loaf of bread, his mother puts a couple of onions, cheese wrapped in butcher paper and a half-rod of winter salami into the wicker basket. His father adds a thermos of milk. His mother covers everything with a dishcloth.

"At least we'll have food on *this* train ride," Gabi's mother says quietly.

Suddenly the grown-ups all stop packing and turn towards her, then each looks at the basket in silence as if it was something very special.

After an early supper, the boys put their bikes in the shed. They cover them with empty potato sacks. They stand shoulder to shoulder in silence. "They look sad," Tomi says.

—

"Hannah, my heart, don't cry," he hears his father say. Tomi stops outside the partially open door. He watches his mother stuff a pouch inside the shoulder lining of her coat. She starts to sew it back up. "I want Magda to come, but she's too far along now. She has another life to think about."

"As do we."

"I almost changed *my* mind, but Magda said no."

"And she will be here for your father."

"But I won't. I feel so guilty and scared about leaving her and my father. I left Faigele and my mother. I'll have no one left."

"Don't you say that, Hannah. You didn't leave Faigele and your mother. They were taken from you. It wasn't your fault. What did your father say?"

"He also thinks we should leave. He says he's too old to try and wants to be buried in his country." She stops sewing and begins to cry again.

"This rotten country doesn't deserve his loyalty," she says.

"They'll be okay." He lifts her chin and wipes her tears away with his fingers and kisses her.

Tomi has never seen his father kiss his mother that way before. They hold each other tight.

"Magda said that she'll come down from Debrecen and watch over our furniture and won't sell it until she hears from us."

"I hope she comes before the neighbours find out we're gone because I'm sure as soon as they do, they'll be all over the place like fleas on a dog."

"Those rotten lice. Just like last time," his mother hisses.

Tomi enters the room quietly and sees his father placing his palms, roof like, above his mother's head. He begins to recite a blessing. Then he kisses her on the forehead. When he sees Tomi, he calls him over and recites the same blessing over him. When Tomi looks up, he sees tears rolling down his father's cheeks. It scares him.

"Everything will be okay," his father says and hugs him hard. They go back to the kitchen where Dezső-papa is setting six shot glasses on the table. He fills each with his homemade pálinka.

"This is a good time for them to take their first drink," he says, handing everyone a glass. "Le Chaim."

Tomi and Gabi look at each other and grin. "Le Chaim," they repeat in unison.

Tomi sniffs the clear liquid. It looks like water but has a sharp, sweet, fruity odour. His grandfather told him that a man becomes a man when he drinks his first glass of pálinka. He shuts his eyes and drinks it down in one shot, the way he saw his father, Dezsö-papa and the other adults do it. He feels nothing. Then his nostrils and throat explode with a burning sensation, as if they are on fire. He is unable to speak and is gasping for air. He tries desperately to blink away the tears forming in his eyes. He forces his eyes open and sees that Gabi's eyes are also open wide and watering. He feels light-headed and dizzy. He grabs hold of the table and waits for the fire to stop burning. It slowly does. How could anybody like this stuff? Why would this make him a man? He takes a deep breath again. Then a slow comforting warmth begins to spread from his head to his toes. He feels as if he is growing taller.

"That'll grow hair on your chest," Dezsö-papa says to the boys. The grown-ups are all smiling. Dezsö pulls Gabi to him and wipes away his tears. Gabi looks at his father and straightens himself.

Tomi's father comes back from the pantry with three more bottles of pálinka and wraps them in separate pieces of cloth, two of which he tucks into the basket.

"No matter what happens, this part of our life is over," his mother says. She turns and leaves the room without looking back. Tomi and his father follow.

"Leave the lights on. Let those hooligans think we're home," his father tells Dezsö-papa, who is the last to leave.

At the door, his father touches his fingers to his lips and then presses them against the hollow cut into the doorpost. "It's where my papa had the mezuzah," he told Tomi once when Tomi saw his father kiss his fingers and put them to that hollow part of the doorframe.

"What's a mezuzah?" he asked his father.

"A mezuzah is a special little box that holds a piece of paper with a prayer written on it to protect the house from bad things.

It's a way that you know a Jewish family lives there. It's the way I met your mother."

"Where'd it go?"

We lost ours during the war."

That was the first time his father ever mentioned that they were Jewish. At that time, Tomi wasn't sure what that meant. Now he knows it means being different, a traitor and Christ killer.

His father lifts Tomi so he can reach the mezuzah. Emma-mama lifts Gabi do the same. Even Dezsö-papa, who made fun of the Jewish cross on the door and called the ritual hocus-pocus, presses his fingers to the hollow. His father closes and locks the door quietly.

His father looks in the blacksmiths' yard. "I wish I could thank them, say a proper goodbye," he says "They're real menschen."

"It's too dangerous, Sanyi," his wife says.

"I know. I won't. I trust them, but it's better this way. I want to leave with a bitter taste in my mouth so I'll never be tempted to return."

He walks over to the bench where the blacksmiths had sat, guarding them every night that week, and lays down a bottle of pálinka.

———

The street is dark and deserted. They're the only ones out, weaving in and out of the side streets.

"It's been like this since they defeated the statue, their first and last great victory," Dezsö-papa says.

"Even the goyim have been staying home."

His father and Dezsö-papa walk in front. Dezsö-papa is wearing his usual sheepskin short coat and riding boots. His father has on his long blood-red leather coat and fedora. The coat is his pride.

"Did you join the Party or the AVO?" Dezsö-papa teased when he saw his father wearing it for the first time.

"I had to do some fancy wheeling and dealing to get it."

His mother and Emma-mama wear their special kerchiefs, the ones from Canada. Their coats are also from Canada. His mother likes telling people that her clothes are from America.

"Don't wear anything too heavy," Emma-mama advised. "I remember how my coat felt like a sack of potatoes last time."

Tomi holds his mother's hand. Something special is happening. He's staying up late, wearing his special-occasion coat and school shoes and they're out. His mother points to the dark streetlamps above them. Most have been smashed. "Hooligans," she says. They walk on in silence, close to the sides of the houses. Shutters are closed tight and most lights are off.

"The town's getting ready for bed," his father says.

"Or trouble."

The houses have an eeriness about them. Even the familiar ones: Small Potato's, Mrs. Tátra's, Carrot's.

As they turn onto Kossuth Street, Tomi hears his mother mutter, "Drop dead!" She's glaring at Mrs. Gombás's house on the corner. She spits. He has never heard her wish such a thing on anybody. He stares up at the darkened windows.

The line, "*The houses too shut their many eyes,*" jumps into his head. I never got to recite it. I practised so much. It's not fair, he thinks to himself. Frog had come by after the recital all excited: "Everybody made mistakes...except me."

Mean old Mrs. Gombás. "Drop dead!" Tomi says under his breath and spits. It makes him feel good and bad.

The coach's house is up ahead. Tomi likes Mr. Varga because he's taught him moves and tricks. "When the time comes, I want Gabi and Tomi on the juvenile team," he said at the practice, before his father was asked not to be scout anymore. "Tomi has the makings of a great soccer player. Maybe another Puskás. You never know."

Tomi had beamed at being compared to Puskás.

Dusk is turning into darkness when they arrive at the train station. Although familiar with it, he's never been there at night.

It's different. The two lampposts, standing like guards on either side of it, light up its edges. But that just makes it scarier. A third light shines on the town sign. Békes is at the end of the line. Here the train turns around to go back to Budapest. The engine is ready to go, steam snorting from its stack. His own breath looks like steam under the station's lights.

He can't believe he's going to Budapest. He remembers Mrs. Gombás telling them that Budapest is one of the great cities of the world. It's special, she told them, because it's really two cities, Buda and Pest, divided by one of the great rivers of the world, the Danube. It's the capital of the great socialist country of the Magyars, she told them. But for Tomi, it is the greatest city in the world because it's where the best soccer players in the world play. And he's going there.

In the waiting room the big clock with its tick-tocking pendulum shows six thirty.

"Sanyi, going back to Budapest tonight? You just got back. And the whole family?" asks Mr. Sipos, the ticket agent and stationmaster. He is also the scorekeeper at the soccer games and Carrot's father.

"Doesn't look like too many people are travelling tonight," Tomi's father says.

"It's a weekday. Not many travel at this time. Only those who have to. People are afraid to travel these days. Not much law and order. Never know who's going to stop the train or blow up the tracks. Only one way? May God be with you," he says as he hands them their tickets. Tomi thinks about Carrot telling him the Jews had killed the Son of God. He'd like to ask Mr. Sipos how he knows that.

The car is empty. His mother and Emma-mama sit by the window facing each other. The boys sit between their parents.

"Look who's getting on board."

"Who?" asks Emma-mama, who is facing away from the door.

"The Baroness and her servant," his mother says.

His mother had begun calling Mrs. Darvas "the Baroness" after their visit to City Hall. Tomi thought that baronesses only existed long, long, long ago.

"Just because her husband is a Party member and they live on Stalin Street, she thinks she's better than us," Tomi had overheard his mother say to Emma-mama.

"She was certainly smart enough to snare him. You don't know because you're not from here, but her father worked for Péter's father before the war and made good money. She was never skinny but not this big when she married him. She's gotten fat from the privileged life," Emma-mama said.

Mrs. Darvas does look like a noble lady in her big fur-collared coat as she marches down the aisle. Mr. Darvas, wearing a coat similar to Tomi's father's but newer, is huffing and puffing behind her. He's carrying two large leather suitcases with a cord attached to the handles that goes around his neck the way Tomi's gloves do. Looking past them, Mrs. Darvas settles into the seat across the aisle. Mr. Darvas nods to his father as he struggles to lift the suitcases onto the overhead rack. Tomi's father and Dezső-papa get up to help.

"Thanks," Mr. Darvas says as he plops himself down across from his wife.

Mrs. Darvas unbuttons her coat, revealing another just like it underneath.

"Why is she wearing two coats?" Tomi asks his mother.

"Maybe she's cold," Gabi answers.

"It's not that cold," Tomi says.

"Because she's a baroness," his mother says in a whisper. Tomi notices his mother and Emma-mama trading smiles as they turn to look out the train window.

"All aboard!" the conductor shouts. Tomi leans over to the window to see the conductor wave his lantern to signal the engineer.

The whistle blows and the train jerks backwards before beginning its slow forward motion. Békes slowly disappears into the darkness.

This is the first time Tomi's ever been on a train. The clack-clack rhythm of the wheels fills his ears. He peers out the window but can't see anything in the darkness. Each stop, with its lit station, comes as a surprise. At every station more people get on. Some are dragging heavy suitcases like Mr. Darvas, but most have only rucksacks on their backs. Most of the people are young, about Fire's age. A few have earlocks like Yossie. There are also people like his parents with kids about his age.

Soon, the car is very crowded, with standing room only. Nobody is smiling. Those who speak, speak quietly. He wonders if everybody is going to Sopron and then to Israel.

He has never been up so late. His usual bedtime is eight o'clock. Now, it is already eleven. And soon, they will be in Budapest. He is excited. He and Gabi will be in Budapest.

"Maybe we'll see the Golden Green. Maybe we'll see a game," Tomi says.

"Don't you remember? They defected."

"Oh, yeah. Stupid defected." Tomi yawns and leans into his mother, who is staring out the window. He sees his and his mother's reflection. It's like there is another Tomi and his mother riding outside the train with them. The rhythm of the train lulls him to sleep.

Hannah gently strokes his brow. In the passing darkness, she sees her reflection and the people behind her. She doesn't like being on crowded trains.

11

The pounding and the shouting scared her awake.

"Open the door. Now!"

The girls, who all slept in one room, ran to their parents' bedroom. "Stay quiet and out of sight," her father commanded. Hannah, Magda and Faigele huddled against the wall in the dark next to their mother.

"Who disturbs the peace at this hour?" Hannah's father asked.

"The Guardians of Silence! Open up now!"

Hannah's father opened the door, blocking the entrance with his pitchfork. Two men in ankle-length leather coats faced him. Behind them stood a man in a black uniform with a large rooster plume sticking out of his black bowler hat.

"Are you Schwartz Moses?"

"Yes."

"You and every Jew in your household are to report to the train station by six o'clock in the morning! One suitcase per person. Do you understand?"

"Why?"

"No questions! Orders!" one of them snapped back. There was silence.

"But we're not Jewish," Moses said. There was a longer moment's silence while the two leather-coated men glanced at each other and consulted the list again.

"Are you or are you not Schwartz Moses?" the man asked again.

"Yes, but we're not Jewish."

"So, why do you have that thing nailed to your doorpost?" He pointed to the mezuzah.

"I have the papers to prove it," Moses said.

"Show me."

How could they not be Jewish? Hannah wondered as her father walked past his wife and daughters, and signalled them to be quiet. He returned with the papers.

"We converted last month," he said.

One officer grabbed the papers and scanned the documents while the other shone his flashlight on them.

"These are no longer valid. All conversions have been annulled," he said curtly. He tore up the papers and tossed the scraps to the night wind.

"Why?" Moses asked.

"No questions. Understand? Do you think you can become a Christian just like that?" the officer shouted. "Do you think you can dirty our religion just like that?" Before they turned to leave, the man with the flashlight drew a large X on the door with a piece of chalk.

"How could you do it?" Hannah's mother asked when her father reappeared.

He sighed and rubbed his face the way he did whenever he came in from the fields after a hard day. "There have been rumours about deportations, about death camps. The wise ones didn't believe them, didn't want to believe them. They said that Hungary was Germany's friend. They wouldn't deport Hungarian Jews. Nobody wanted to believe that deportations and concentration camps existed. Too impossible, they said. But I believed the rumours. I know. I've seen with my own eyes what men can do to each other. I know there is evil in this world. I know there is evil in men's hearts, waiting for a chance to leap out and devour. I remembered the White Terror pogroms after the Great War. So I went to City Hall and officially converted the family. I thought, if God was as wise and compassionate as the rabbis say He is, then He would understand and would know that in my heart I was still a Jew."

"But it's a sin to abandon our faith, especially in times like this," she said.

"I know. But I didn't abandon our faith. I converted for now. I still pray to our God. I still keep His commandments. And what I did, I did alone. God won't punish you or the children for my actions. The rabbis tell us His ways are mysterious, and it is not for us to know why He made His chosen people such scapegoats. And if it is His command that I, like Abraham, am to bring my children to His altar for sacrifice, I will, but I know that these men are not God's angels and I don't see this as His test of our faith."

Faigele, Hannah's younger sister, had her arms wrapped around her mother's waist. Like a mother hen trying to protect and comfort her brood, Sara embraced the children. "What are we going to do?"

Moses Schwartz was well-versed in the Torah and the commentaries; he always had a prayer or a saying for every occasion. But now, as he looked at them he was silent. Finally, he spoke with quiet resignation. "The Lord will fight for you."

When morning came, Moses stepped in front of his wife, made a roof with his two palms over her head, and prayed. "May God make you like Sara, Rebecca, Rachel and Leah," he intoned. "May God bless you and watch over you. May God shine His face toward you and show you favour. May God grant you peace."

When he finished, he kissed her on the forehead and hugged her. He did the same to each of his daughters, from eldest to youngest: Magda, Hannah and Faigele. His tears touched each of them.

"Go and pack your warmest clothes. Sara, give each of them bread and boiled eggs to carry." Moses went out to the barn and when he came back he gave each of them five individual gold chain links.

"Your father's watch chain," Sara cried.

"I want you to hide them where they won't find them. Use them only when you have nothing else to trade."

The girls went back to their room. Hannah and Faigele started to cry. "Stop it," Magda snapped at them. "Start packing!"

"But we don't have suitcases," Hannah said.

"Wrap your clothes in a tablecloth."

"Where should we hide the gold?" Faigele asked.

"Like papa said, where they won't find it," Magda said. Hannah and Faigele stared at Magda.

"Where babies come from," she said.

Hannah looked at her sister in disbelief.

"Where do babies come from?" Faigele asked.

"Where you make peepee," Magda said. "Wrap them in a little cloth and put it in your underwear."

Hannah also took her book, *Les Misérables*.

"Where are we going? What's going to happen to us?" Faigele asked as she looked at their small bundles on the floor. Her mother came in before Magda needed to answer.

"Come, girls. Try to get some sleep," she said and lay down with Faigele. Hannah lay beside Magda. Magda hugged Hannah tightly. They fell asleep to their father's praying.

On their way out the next morning, one by one they put their fingers to their lips and then to the mezuzah on the doorpost. Her father walked in front, her mother held Faigele's hand, and Magda and Hannah, arm in arm, followed. They crossed the commons and joined the other families heading toward the station. Hannah looked back and saw the neighbours standing in their doorways, watching in silence.

The small station was already filled with many of the Jewish families from Szabad and the surrounding farms. The place was abuzz with confusion, fear and crying.

"No talking!" shouted black-shirted men wearing armbands of the Arrow Cross.

Officers and soldiers with growling dogs began to separate the men from the women and herd them into separate cattle cars.

Hannah lost sight of her father and tried to dart out of her group to find him, but Magda grabbed her before the soldiers saw.

"Don't," she said, squeezing Hannah's arm.

"Hold hands, don't get separated," Magda whispered to Hannah and Faigele. She made sure that the girls and their mother all got into the same wagon. The door slammed shut. The only light that came into the overcrowded wagon was through the knotholes and the broken slats that reached out to poke them like bony fingers. There was much wailing and shouting. Hannah shivered and cried out, "Papa! Help!"

Magda and her mother reached out to her. A sharp whistle pierced the crying and wailing. The train lurched forward, slamming everyone into each other.

12

"Tomi, wake up, we're here."

He groans and stretches. Rubbing his eyes, he looks out the window. It's filled with pinpricks of light.

"We're here. We're in Budapest," his mother says.

The people in the car are trying to collect their suitcases and bags as fast as possible. They are bumping each other, urging each other to move, to hurry and to watch it. Some are shoving their suitcases out the train windows, some are dragging them along the floor. To Tomi, they seem to be rushing as if they're hearing some terrible voice shouting, cracking a whip.

"Let's wait," his mother says.

His father helps Mr. Darvas take down the suitcases. "Sanyi, handle them carefully," Mrs. Darvas commands. "They're valuable."

"Yes, your Baroness," He hears his father say under his breath.

Tomi sees Mr. Darvas smile. "Thanks, Sanyi," he says.

"Péter, hurry up!" Mrs. Darvas squawks, elbowing her way to the front.

"Look! It's got a glass roof!" Gabi shouts as he cranes his neck to see all the way up to the top of the station.

"It's a glass palace for trains!"

"Look at all these trains! I already counted eight!"

"I bet there are more people in the station than all the people in Hajdúbékes."

Tomi takes Gabi's hand. Loudspeakers are announcing arrivals and departures, people are waving and yelling and conductors are blowing whistles. The hissing engines blast large puffs of steam. Tomi feels like he's in the land of loud, tree-crushing giants and dragons.

"Gabi, look. Soldiers."

Tomi's mother grabs his hand and squeezes hard.

"Ouch."

"Budapest is free! Hungary is free!" They salute, smile and continue on.

"Sanyi! Sanyi!" a voice calls from the crowd.

"Ernö!" he shouts back, waves. When the man reaches them, he and Tomi's father shake hands.

"This is Ernö Lakatos," his father introduces him to the others.

"This is not what we agreed on, Sanyi," Ernö says as he looks at Dezsö-papa, Emma-mama and Gabi.

"Things have changed."

"I don't think she will…"

"We'll pay you," Dezsö-papa says.

"But there is only room for three."

"We've shared before. We'll manage."

"She'll want more."

"I said we'll pay."

"I'm not promising anything. She might not go for this change. If she doesn't, you're on your own."

"Agreed," says Tomi's father.

"Now, let's get you your tickets for Sopron."

"How do we know that there'll be a train tomorrow?" Dezsö-papa asks.

"You don't, but in case there is, it's better this way. Tomorrow you'll have to stand in line and fight for them."

His father pulls out some money and hands it over to Ernö, who disappears into the crowd.

"Can we trust this guy?" Dezsö-papa asks. "I've had bad experiences with people like him."

"Yes, we can. He met us, didn't he? He had our money. He could just as well have not shown up."

"I don't mean only that."

They stand in silence. Tomi watches the people around him. Everything, everyone seems to be moving so much faster than in Békes. He feels that the people in Békes are turtles compared to people here. Ernö returns with their tickets.

"Let's go. It's not far from here."

The huge station clock shows twelve thirty. Tomi has never in his whole life been up this late. Even though it's the middle of the night, there are people everywhere he looks. He has never seen so many people on a street in Békes, not even after a soccer game. Grown-ups and kids his age are walking along the street, talking loudly and smiling, as if it were a Saturday night. Many of them are wearing green, white and red armbands and many have rifles, like the hunters he's seen around Békes; others have pistols strapped to their waists. Boys and girls with slingshots and sticks are laughing, shouting and running in and out of alleys.

"Everybody looks happy. They seem to be having fun," Emma-mama says.

"For how long?" Dezsö-papa asks.

"Why do the flags have the middle cut out of them?" Gabi asks his father.

"So people can see what's on the other side."

"Sanyi, have you heard the news? The Russians have withdrawn from Budapest," Mr. Lakatos says. "Hungary is going to be free. You sure you still want to go?"

"We've had enough," his mother says. Her face is very serious. Since the night of the mob, she has been more and more angry.

Mr. Lakatos leads the way along winding and cobblestoned streets. Tomi has never seen so many houses stuck together and so high. The streets curve like snakes and keep getting narrower. And there are so many streetlights. As they pass beneath each one, his shadow sneaks up from behind, disappears when he is right under it, then appears and starts to grow in front of him. He counts the steps between lampposts. After a while they're further apart and the streets are darker and quieter. The snaking seems to go on forever. He's getting tired. "Will we be there soon?" he asks. His father picks him up.

"Soon," he says.

Finally they stop in front of a large building.

"We're here," Mr. Lakatos says. "Stand near the wall, out of the light."

Tomi counts five levels of windows. In Békes, only a few houses are more than one storey. Only City Hall has three floors. The walls of these houses have cracks like veins running in all directions and large chunks of plaster missing, just like the synagogue in Békes.

Mr. Lakatos pulls on a cord and a bell clangs somewhere far away inside the building. He looks up and down the dark and deserted street. It just seems to disappear into the darkness at both ends.

"Who is it that disturbs the peace?" a crackly old woman's voice asks from behind the door with a lion's head that has a ring through its nose. It looks and sounds like it's the lion speaking.

"Good evening, Mrs. Jonás. I am here with the guests." Mr. Lakatos waves to them to stand in front of the door. A light over the door comes on and part of the door slides open. A pair of eyes appears in the slit. They move darting from side to side, like a cat checking out its prey. The peephole slides shut. Then a bolt clacks and a lock turns.

"Who is she?" Gabi asks. "She looks scary."

"Mrs. Jonás is the concierge of the building. She's nice."

"What's a concierge?" Tomi asks.

"A concierge is a person in charge of who's let in and who's not," his father says.

"They're snoops and spies," Dezsö-papa adds. "They report anyone they don't like to the police."

Emma-mama yanks at Dezsö-papa's sleeve. "Don't scare the children."

The door creaks open. An old woman eyes them suspiciously. The candle she is holding lights up her wrinkled face. Tomi is sure that she's a witch. Tomi and Gabi slip closer to their mothers.

"It's late," she says.

"We're sorry, but the train was late," Tomi's father says. He clasps her hand with both of his. Dezsö-papa does the same. She looks at her palm. She nods and smiles.

"Follow me." Slowly, she leads them up three flights. The stairs and the hallways are dark; it smells like their root cellar. He reaches out to touch the wall as he climbs. It's slimy. The candle casts eerie shadows as they climb. At each landing, Mrs. Jonás has to stop to catch her breath. Finally, they stop in front of a door. She taps quietly.

"Yes?" a very quiet voice calls from behind the door.

"They're here."

A lock turns and then a bolt. The door opens slightly and a woman's pale face peeks out. She looks at them for a minute in silence. "Ernö. You said three."

"They're willing to pay."

The pale face disappears and the door closes. They wait. A few seconds later, it opens.

"Good evening. Please come in."

Mrs. Jonás lets out a loud sigh and hobbles back down the stairs.

"Mrs. Aranyi, this is Sándor and Hannah Wolfstein and Dezsö and Emma Földember." He turns to them. "Sanyi, I have to go now, but I'll see you tomorrow in Sopron."

They stand huddled in the entrance of the apartment, Tomi holding his mother's hand tightly.

"Please come in. And what is your name?" she asks Gabi. "And yours?" she turns to Tomi. They whisper their names. This apartment is bigger and has more rooms than their house in Békes.

"Would you like some tea?"

"Thank you, but we don't want to bother you," Tomi's mother says.

"No bother." Mrs. Aranyi goes to the small kitchen and turns a knob on the stove. A ring of blue flame pops up.

"What's that?" Tomi asks.

"It's a gas stove," his mother explains. "They use gas instead of wood to cook."

He wonders how it burns without wood and in such a perfect circle.

They all move into the sitting room, which is stuffed with a sofa, a table with short legs and a glass cabinet filled with porcelain figurines, the kind Emma-mama loves, of ballet dancers and little shepherd boys playing flutes. There is hardly any room to run around. On the other side of the sitting room are three closed doors.

"One family can have this one. This is my son's. He's away." She opens one of the doors and switches on the light.

Seeing the double bed, Hannah turns to Mrs. Aranyi. "We'll put the children there and we'll sit on the sofa."

Mrs. Aranyi looks at the children and then at his mother. "No. Children should not be separated from parents in strange places. You can have my bed, I will take the sofa."

"Thank you very much. You are very kind." His mother looks less serious than he has seen her in a while. She is smiling. Gabi and Emma-mama go to one room while Tomi and his mother wait for his father, who is giving some money to Mrs Aranyi.

Tomi tugs at his mother's sleeve. "I have to go to the bathroom."

Mrs. Aranyi points to the third door. "Over there."

Tomi looks at his mother and pinches his nose. "In the house?" His father has spoken of bathrooms in buildings, but he always thought he was joking.

His mother rises and he follows her to the bathroom, fully expecting it to be smelly and buzzing with flies like their outhouse. When she opens the door, though, he doesn't smell anything bad or see a swarm of flies.

It has a porcelain chair with a wooden ring around it and a tank above it with a dangling chain.

"You have to pull the chain once you're finished," his mother tells him.

"Why?"

"Because it flushes away the pee."

"But it will fall on the people below."

"No, it goes through pipes down to the ground."

"Really?"

"Yes."

"Wow!"

His mother is smiling. He's amazed and happy that he doesn't have to walk down three dark flights, go outside to the back of a strange yard, and be spied on by the concierge.

He hesitates before he pulls the chain. What if the tank falls down and hits him on the head? What if the water spills out when he pulls the chain? He closes his eyes and pulls. He hears a swoosh as water flows into the toilet. He opens his eyes and jumps back and runs out.

On one wall of the son's room, facing the bed, is a painting of Hussars on horseback, their swords drawn and capes flying. They're galloping across the plains. The window next to the bed is large and even this late has light shining in. It looks out on the street that they just came from. The lampposts look like sunflowers after the sun sets, with their heads bent as if they have just nodded off. Their lights flicker on and off like huge fireflies.

"Get ready for bed," his mother says.

Undressing, he notices a row of four photographs on the wall opposite the window. The nearest one is a picture of a soldier looking very serious. The next one is of the same soldier holding hands with a girl. The third is of him again with his soldier buddies, their arms around each other's shoulders. In the last picture, he is sitting in the gun turret of a tank, gripping a machine gun and smiling.

Although he has never seen a real one, tanks are one of Tomi's favourite things. He cuts pictures of them out of newspapers and magazines. He loves drawing them. Gabi taught him how to draw them using a ruler and a penny. In his drawings, the hatch is always up and there is always a soldier sitting there gripping a machine gun, just like the soldier in the photo on the wall. The gunner is always firing the machine gun.

He and Gabi also make tanks out of small matchboxes. They use matches for the barrel because the red tips make them look like they are firing.

Just as he's about to run to tell Gabi that he's sleeping in a tank gunner's room, his mother grabs him by the shoulder. "Don't run. It's very late. Take off your shoes and walk quietly. There are people below us."

He places his shoes under the bed and tiptoes to the next room. "Hey, Gabi. Guess what?"

"What?"

He whispers as if he's revealing a big secret. "There are people below us and I'm sleeping in a tank gunner's room."

"Oh, yeah?" Gabi yawns and crawls under the duvet.

Tomi is crawling into bed when he notices a cross over the bed. It has a man almost naked with his arms outstretched on the cross. Tomi looks closer. He has nails in his hands. He's looking up to the ceiling. He looks like he's in pain. Tomi reaches out to make sure that his parents are on either side of him.

Lying between his parents, staring at the ceiling, he thinks about all the things that have happened lately. Not so long ago people in Békes were nice, but now they aren't. Now they want to hurt his family because they're Jewish. Only a week ago he was in school preparing to recite his poem for a nice teacher who liked him, but then she didn't and threw him out of class. A few days ago he had a shiny new bike and now he doesn't. Just a few hours ago he was in Békes and now he is in Budapest, the biggest city in the country, the city of his favourite soccer team, in a soldier's bed, in a strange house with blue flames and an indoor bathroom and Christ above his head.

I'm sorry that we killed you, he thinks to himself, as he drifts off to sleep and wonders how long the train ride to Israel will take. He hopes that they play soccer there.

NOVEMBER

.

1956

13

The growling-rumbling grows louder and louder. It sounds familiar. He opens his eyes, but it's dark and he can't see. The rumbling is getting nearer. He feels his whole body vibrating. There is something on his face. Like a puffy hand. He reaches up to push it away. He yanks off the duvet. Light hits him in the face. He's in a strange room.

"Sanyi! Quick! Come here!"

His parents are at the window in the sitting room. He scrambles out of bed to join them. "It's a tank! It's a real tank!" It's at the end of the street and it's rumbling towards them! It's huge. It takes up the width of the street.

Gabi and his parents are at the window now too.

"The Russians are back," Dezsö-papa says. "I knew they wouldn't stay away."

Unlike Tomi's drawings, this tank doesn't have the big red star painted on its front. It has a white stripe running from front to back. Also, its hatch is closed. It looks like some giant hound, its claws ripping up the cobblestones as it advances up the street.

Out of nowhere, a group of young boys and girls run out into the middle of the street.

"Oh, no." His mother reaches for Tomi. "What in God's name are those children doing? The tank will crush them."

The children hold their ground and the tank comes to a slow, grinding halt. The tank and the children face each other.

"David and Goliath," his father says.

A boy darts out from an alley, and, like a spider, scurries up the side of the tank. He reaches into his pocket, pulls out a fistful of something and smears it across the peephole. It all happens in a flash. He jumps off and the children scatter in different directions. The street is deserted again. Only the idling motor of the tank can be heard.

Mesmerized, Tomi watches. At first nothing seems to be happening. Then, like a mouth yawning, the hatch opens.

A hand pushes up the cover and quickly withdraws. A few minutes later, little by little, a leather-helmeted, goggled half-head appears. Like a groundhog peeping out of its hole, it nervously jerks from side to side, up and around, and then quickly ducks back down. The hatch stays open. A minute or so later, the head reappears and this time stays. It rotates slowly. Soon, other parts of the soldier: neck, shoulders, torso starts to appear. The gunner settles in his turret, but before he can grip the handles of the machine gun the street's silence is broken by bursts of gunfire.

Tomi sees puffs of smoke from rooftops and windows. Popping sounds are everywhere. A hand pushes him down and a body lands on him. The air rushes out of him. He can hardly breathe. He tries to cry out, but he can't.

The firing stops, but the body on top of him doesn't move. "Mama," he manages to grunt, while in panic he tries to wiggle out from under the weight. But it's impossible. "Mama! Papa!" he cries." The weight lifts. He turns his head to look. His mother is on her knees, still bent over him.

"Hannah! Tomi! Are you okay?"

"Gabi! Emma!" Dezsö-papa turns towards them.

"Yes, we're okay," the mothers say.

Trying to get his breath back, Tomi watches his father and Dezsö-papa slowly raise their heads to look out the window.

"What's going on?"

"God," his father cries out.

"What?" Emma asks.

His mother also raises her head to look. "Oh my God."

Tomi stands and sees the gunner slumped over his gun. Two boys run toward the tank, each carrying a bottle with flaming rags sticking out of them. "What are they doing?" Tomi asks. One climbs up onto the tank and drops his lit bottle into the turret, closes the hatch cover, jumps down and runs off. The other rolls his bottle under the tank and he too disappears.

A loud explosion rocks the street as the tank blows up from inside out. Like a popped cork, the hatch cover flies up into the air. Flames shoot out of the turret and the tank barrel, rising almost as high as their apartment window.

Everybody jerks back from the window. "God!" his mother shrieks.

Tomi's heart is racing. His body shakes. He is breathing hard. In a daze, he stands. "Get down!" his mother yells. Just then, another explosion. The window panes shatter and shards of glass fly into the apartment, scattering everywhere.

"We have to get out of here!" his mother screams.

"Mama! Mama!" Tomi cries as he falls to his knees with his palms to his face. Blood is seeping through his fingers.

"Oh God! Oh God!" She grabs him by the wrists, trying to get his hands away from his face. "Let me see! Let me see! Take your hands away!" she shouts but Tomi won't let go.

"Let me see!" She yanks his hands away. They're smeared with blood.

"Ow! Ow!"

Tomi feels warm liquid seeping down his brow, trickling down his face. It's in his eyes. He tries to rub them but his mother is holding his wrists firmly.

"Don't touch your face!" she says. Tomi can't see her but he hears the panic in her voice.

"Ow. You're hurting me!" he cries. "Don't hurt me! I can't see! I can't see!"

"Sanyi! Take him out of here!"

His father scoops him up and runs to the kitchen.

"Be careful!" Mrs. Aranyi shouts. "There's glass all over the floor."

"It hurts. It hurts," Tomi wails.

Mrs. Aranyi looks at Tomi. "Sit there and hold him," she says to Sanyi.

Through his blurry eyes, Tomi sees Mrs. Aranyi's face lean in close. "Don't open your eyes!" she barks at him. He shrinks back from her and closes his eyes.

"Mama! I want my mama!"

Mrs. Aranyi places her palm gently on his head. "Now, Tomi, don't move." She speaks quietly but sternly.

He freezes. She runs her fingers softly over his scalp, then over his face.

"Ow."

She strokes his arms.

"Ow! It hurts! It hurts!"

"Don't let him touch his arms or face. There are slivers everywhere. We'll have to pull them out. I'll be right back."

"Don't let her pull out my eyes!" Tomi screams.

"She won't, my darling! We won't. It's just some small pieces of glass. We have to take them out."

Mrs. Aranyi returns with tweezers, some cotton balls, a little brown bottle and a roll of gauze.

"Let me handle this," she says. "I used to be a nurse."

"No! It's going to hurt," Tomi cries, struggling to pull free.

"No, it won't. Hannah, hold his wrists. Sanyi, you hold his head by the chin and top. Don't let him move his head. Tomi, keep your eyes closed but not tight. Like you're lying in your bed waiting to go to sleep. That's a good boy. Breathe slowly and deeply."

A gentle finger slides very lightly over his eyelids. It feels like butterflies.

"Good, there are no slivers there. I'm just going to wipe them with a damp cotton ball. "Good. Now, Tomi open your eyes slowly. Good." She looks him in the eyes. "You are a brave boy. Now I'm going to take out the slivers from your brow, cheeks and arms. Don't move. Understand?"

His parents look really worried. He can't speak or nod because his father is holding his head rigid. He opens and closes his eyelids slowly a couple of times.

"Good." She kneels and works quickly, plucking out the slivers.

Tomi bites his lip, balls his fingers into fists and tightens his jaw more tightly each time she plucks out a sliver.

"What a brave boy," she says dabbing his face with the moist cotton ball. "Okay, now your arms."

"See?" Mrs. Aranyi says, holding out a palmful of slivers, "It's all over."

"Please make sure there aren't any left," Gabi's mother says. "We don't want infections."

"Sanyi, hold him steady while I pour some iodine over his cheeks and arms."

Tomi howls. The raw sting is unbearable. It hurts more than the plucking.

"It's okay, it's okay. You'll be okay," Mrs. Aranyi says, blowing softly over the cuts to cool the stinging. She takes another cotton ball and gently dabs it against his cheek and arms.

Tomi is shaking.

"He looks pale," Emma-mama says.

The way everybody is staring at him frightens Tomi. He takes shallow gulps of air, struggling to catch his breath.

Mrs. Aranyi opens his eyelids wide with her fingers and looks into his eyes. "A little shock, but he'll be okay. Tomi, I want you to take big deep breaths, like this," she says, breathing with him as she winds the gauze around his arms. "It's okay," she says softly. "You'll be better in a minute."

"Lift his arm up to slow the bleeding," Dezső-papa says.

"Here is some water. Drink it," Mrs. Aranyi hands him a glass.

"Everything's going to be okay. Everything is going to be okay," his mother repeats as she holds out her arms to him. Her eyes are softer now but her jaw is clenched. He sits on her lap.

As he leans into her she lets out a shuddering sigh and begins to gently rock him.

His father flashes Tomi a broad smile. "How are you?"

"It really hurts," he says between breaths. "It really, really, really hurts."

"Wow! Your face looks like it's full of red freckles. You're a brave wounded soldier—like Nemecsek," Gabi says with a hint of envy. Tomi looks at him, sniffles a couple of times, takes a deep breath and manages a wan smile.

"I didn't cry."

———

His father goes back to the window and looks out. "We have to go," he says.

"We can't, not now." Emma-mama protests. "It's too dangerous."

"Emma, it's more dangerous to stay. How long do you think these people can hold out against the Russians?" Dezsö-papa asks. "The Ruskies are going to come here with more tanks and arrest or kill everybody."

"Where can we go? The train doesn't leave until tonight."

"Dohány Street," his father says without hesitation.

Mrs. Aranyi comes out of the kitchen with a tray of sliced bread and jam and puts it on the little table. "Eat before you go," she says. "You don't know when you'll have a chance again. The children need to eat something." She goes back to the kitchen and returns with cups of milk for each of them.

"Thank you. You are really kind, Mrs. Aranyi," his mother says.

"Those kids were really brave," Gabi says as he chews on a piece of bread and sips his milk.

"I got wounded," Tomi touches his cheek and rubs his arm.

"Does it hurt?"

"Not too much. What happened to the tank? Why did it explode like that?"

"The kids threw Molotov cocktails into the tank," Gabi's father answered.

"What are Molotov cocktails?" Gabi asks.

"They are the proletariat's hand grenade, a good use of an empty pálinka bottle," Dezsö-papa says. He sounds like he's happy.

Tomi remembers that he was drinking the pálinka before they left Békes. And, now, he's been wounded. He's pretty sure that now he's a man.

"They definitely accomplished the job," his father says.

"Yeah, they blew up those damned Ruskies good!"

"Dezsö! They're *children!*"

"So were we once. So are those little soldiers. There's no time to be a child in these times."

"My son is a tank gunner," Mrs. Aranyi says quietly.

Tomi's mother goes to Mrs. Aranyi and embraces her. They hold each other tightly. Tomi thinks his mother looks like a little girl in her arms.

After a few moments, Mrs. Aranyi pulls away. "You'd better go now."

When they've gathered their belongings, Mrs. Aranyi kneels and hugs the boys. "You be brave now," she says to each of them. "Good-bye and good luck. God keep you safe."

"You too," Tomi's mother says, tears welling in her eyes.

Tomi reaches out to his mother. "Don't cry, Mama. Hold my hand."

Mrs. Jonás is waiting for them at the gate. She doesn't look as frightening now. "God keep you safe," she says, locking the door behind them.

Waves of heat hit them as they step into the street. The smell of burning fuel and something else that is strange to Tomi ride the waves of heat. The acrid smell fills their nostrils and throats. His mother gags. Tomi and Gabi begin to cough.

"Here, hold these handkerchiefs to your mouth," his mother says.

A crowd has gathered around the smouldering tank. Some people are holding handkerchiefs to their faces, like Tomi and Gabi. A plume of smoke drifts up over the crowd. Chunks of metal, big and small, litter the cobblestones. Pieces of the tank are sticking out of doors and walls. Kids are running around filling their pockets with bits of the exploded tank. Tomi looks around for scraps.

He steps in something wet. He looks down and sees dark liquid is oozing from the middle of the crowd. It's coming from the blown-up tank. Tomi didn't think that a tank could be blown up. He thought they were invincible. They never got blown up in their games.

The oil snakes through the legs of the crowd leaving a dark slimy winding trail around the broken cobblestones. It flows toward the gutter, where it becomes a coppery, metallic blue-gold and reddish pool before disappearing down the drain.

Tomi can see a Hungarian flag, the kind with the hole in its centre, stuck into the tank's barrel. It reminds him of a picture of a dragon pierced by a knight's lance.

Tomi is surprised that the people gathered seem so happy. Some of them are cheering and laughing, while others are just smiling and chatting to each other.

"Hurry," Tomi's father says and pushes his way through the crowd, past the blown-up tank. He heads down the street. Tomi's mother, Gabi, Emma-mama and Dezsö-papa follow. "Stick close to the wall," his father calls out to his mother as he leads them away from the crowd.

Tomi presses against the wall. "Ow." He rubs his shoulder.

"Don't touch it. It'll only make it worse," his mother says.

Tomi kicks at the bits of cobblestone dislodged by the explosions. He aims his kicks, like Puskás, to different parts of the street. One of them feels soft against his instep. When he looks down, he sees a dark shiny stain on his school shoes.

—

As they turn a corner Emma-mama looks up at the street sign and stops, a smile spreading over her face. "It's Rákóczi Street," she says almost reverently. She looks down the street and points, "Look, the National Theatre. I wanted to go there."

"Look how wide the street is!" Gabi spreads his arms. "As wide as a soccer field."

They pass stores with smashed windows, walk around overturned café tables and chairs. The walls are plastered with large posters. "Looks like Jóska." Tomi points to a poster of a muscular man with a hammer raised over his head, about to strike. Another is of a sword rising out of a mountain toward the sky, towards a glowing sun. Like his sword. He hopes no one has found it. Another shows men and women marching and holding a huge Hungarian flag with its middle cut out. The familiar posters with the hammer and sickle have had black paint thrown over them or are torn, their loose edges flapping in the sharp November wind.

Tomi reads the hand-painted signs out loud. "Ruskies Go Home!"

"Sure. Maybe if we say 'Please,'" Dezsö-papa snorts.

"Freedom!" Gabi points to a poster across the street. Another poster, without a picture, just one word on it, catches Tomi's eye. Slowly, letter by letter, he tries to sound it out. "H, E, L, P." He's never heard that word before. "What does that one say?"

His father pauses and stares as if remembering something. "It's an American word. It means help," his father says.

"You speak American?"

"Look," Gabi points. Men and women with rifles are hiding behind overturned trucks, derailed streetcars and another blown-up tank. A couple of blocks further they see a group of men and women gathered around a barrel that has fire flaming out of it. They are laughing and throwing Russian flags and posters of Stalin, Marx and Lenin into it.

"Let's hurry," his father urges. Tomi has to almost run to keep up. His father picks him up and begins to walk faster.

"Ow!"

"I'm sorry," his father says, kissing his wounded arm. "Hold on tight," his father says and turns down a side street. "This way," he calls to the others.

The street is narrow and deserted. It's quiet. The walls are pockmarked. Some of buildings have shiny bullets in them. Tomi reaches out to try to grab one.

"Slow down," Sanyi orders the group.

Two people with rifles slung over their shoulders are coming towards them. As they near, Tomi sees that they are holding hands.

They smile. "Freedom, patriots! Freedom!" They raise their joined arms and walk on.

"A girl soldier," Gabi says.

"She had a rifle," Tomi says, rubbing his wounded arm.

They turn a corner. "Here we are," his father says.

Tomi reads the street sign out loud. "Dohány Street."

14

"Once upon a time, a long long long…"

"…time ago!"

"…Jews were not allowed to live in Budapest."

"Why not?"

"It was the law. So they lived just outside the city, on the other side of the wall that surrounded Pest. And there they built a big beautiful synagogue, so big that all the Jews of Hungary could fit into it. And people from around the world came to admire it."

"Why?"

"Because it was beautiful."

"It's a sultan's palace!" Gabi shouts. "Just like the one in my *Ali Baba* book."

"It's as big as a soccer field."

"Bigger," says his father.

"It's as tall as the sky!"

Tomi looks up at the two towers that rise on either side of a large arched doorway.

"Look! Six-sided towers."

"Round windows and square windows on top of them."

"Look, golden onions on top."

"They look like six-eyed guards with turbans."

"Can you see the Ten Commandment tablets?" his father asks him, pointing to the two plaques between the domes.

"They're as big as doors."

The large front gate has a small door inside it. His father grasps the large iron ring and knocks three times. He waits and then knocks three more times. Soon, the peephole opens and a pair of nervous eyes peeks out. Tomi wonders if every door in Budapest has these peepholes and why people are so scared here. In Békes, nobody he knew locked their doors, at least not until recently.

"Yes?"

"Zev Yankov ben shmiel Yisroel," his father says.

"What did he say?"

"That's your father's Jewish name," his mother says.

The door opens. A short elderly man with a big grey beard and bushy moustache is standing before them. For a moment, Tomi thinks it's Rabbi Stern.

"Shalom."

"Shalom," his father replies.

"Just like in *Ali Baba!*"

"In *Ali Baba* he says 'sesame.' How come Papa's name opened the door?"

"I'll tell you later." His mother is smiling.

"Do I have a Jewish name too?"

"Of course."

"What is it?"

"Zev Avram ben Yankov."

"Does it open doors?"

"Some."

"This one?"

"Yes. But shush now." She nudges him in through the door.

"Hey, Gabi, my name opens doors."

Once they're inside, the place seems even bigger. Tomi and Gabi have to tilt their heads back to see all the way up to the ceiling, where yellowish grey rays shine through a stained-glass skylight.

"They look like monster grapes," Tomi says, pointing to the clusters of lights hanging from the high ceiling.

"I want to go up there." Gabi points to the balconies that run along both sides.

"No. You can fall down from there," Emma-mama says in a hushed voice.

They walk down the aisle between the dark shiny pews, which are filled with people huddled in clumps, families like his, with bags and suitcases. He recognizes a few faces from the train. Some of the men nod to his father. His father and mother nod back and smile. Even though there are many people in the synagogue, it is so big that it doesn't look crowded. A plaintive song floats from the front. Someone is singing.

"Here." His father points to an empty row. Maybe his father hadn't been exaggerating. Maybe all the Jews of Hungary *could* fit in here. He looks around, feeling very small.

"We can stay until it's time to go the station. We're safe here," his father says.

—

"I'm hungry," Gabi says.

"Me too," Tomi says.

They haven't eaten since early morning and it is now past noon.

"All right, I'll prepare some food." Emma-mama reaches into her basket and pulls out the winter salami.

"No!" Tomi's father pushes the salami back into the basket.

"What's wrong?" Emma asks.

"It's not kosher."

"So?" Dezsö asks.

"We're in a synagogue."

"Food is food. I don't care if it's kosher or not. Who knows the difference?"

"I do."

"Your stomach doesn't mind being fed unkosher salami at home."

"This is God's house."

"All right, then, give it to me and I'll circumcise it," Dezsö says.

"Dezsö!" Emma-mama reprimands him, but she's smiling. It's the kind of smile that she has before she starts to laugh at one of his father's jokes. Tomi likes that Emma-mama is happy. It makes him feel better.

"All right, but if He didn't want us to eat unkosher food, why did He make unkosher animals? Tell me that, Sanyi."

Tomi too wonders why Christians are allowed to eat everything and they aren't. And when he ate bacon with the blacksmiths he didn't feel less Jewish.

Dezsö-papa is always saying things that make Tomi's father uneasy. And it's usually about religion. Most of the time the questions seem to make sense. His father's answers tend to be like Rabbi Stern's—"We aren't smart enough" or "God's ways are mysterious"—although he doesn't sound as convincing as Rabbi Stern.

But his father doesn't answer Dezsö-papa now. He just gives him a hard look.

"All right." Emma-mama sighs, digs back into the basket and takes out a pogácsa and a boiled egg for each boy. "Here. Eat slowly and take small bites." His mother slices pieces of cheese slivers of onions. His father fills the thermos cap with milk. The boys take turns drinking. "Careful not to spill."

"Yes, be careful because there are no cows in Budapest," Dezsö says.

"Sanyi, we're going to need some food for tonight and for later."

"There's a market nearby. I'll go see what I can get."

"I'll go with you," Dezsö-papa says.

Tomi is happy that his father and Dezsö-papa aren't angry with each other anymore.

"What should I get?"

"Rock candy!" Gabi cries out.

"Puh-lease!"

"Sure," his mother smiles. "And bread, and anything else that's easy to carry and will keep for a day or two."

"How about apples?" Emma says. "They're oh-so-delicious at this time of the year!"

"Maybe some iodine and some gauze too if you can find a drugstore. Be careful and hurry back."

His mother reaches up and embraces his father. He has never seen her hug him like that before. It looks like she doesn't want to let him go.

"We'll be back soon," Gabi's father promises, kissing Emma-mama and Gabi.

There's a lot of kissing and hugging going on lately, Tomi thinks.

—

"Can we explore?" Tomi asks.

"It would be nice to walk around a bit," Gabi's mother says, looking at Hannah.

"You're right. When will we get another chance to see this beautiful place again? Don't run!" she calls out before they even have a chance to take off.

The four of them walk slowly down the aisle. "Look at the little balconies," Tomi says, pointing to the fancy pulpits on either side.

"You climb that one," Gabi says, pointing to the one on the left.

"No!" the mothers cry out, but the boys are already halfway up. They wave to each other.

He makes believe he's the captain of a ship. "Hello out there!" His voice echoes across the synagogue to Gabi.

"Goodbye out there!" Gabi shouts back.

"Get down," Tomi's mother orders through clenched teeth.

The old man who let them in hurries over, wagging his finger at them. "No! No! That's only for the cantor and the rabbi."

Emma-mama bows her head apologetically. "I'm sorry, we're not from here. They haven't seen anything like this before."

"Get down! Now!" Tomi's mother repeats in a hoarse whisper.

Reluctantly, they climb down. Tomi's mother yanks him while Emma-mama grabs Gabi's ear. They both yelp.

"See what happens when you don't obey?"

"My arm," Tomi cries out.

Gabi's mother raises her hand but stops in mid-air. "Act grown up. Walk properly. You aren't an animal! Behave! You're in a holy place."

The boys shuffle to the front with their heads down. They sneak look at each other and grin. They stop in the front and look at the ark. "Rabbi Stern's Torah cupboard could fit two times into this!"

"Three times."

"Look." Tomi points to the large Star of David on the purple curtain. He strokes it "It's so soft. Like a kitten." The star is surrounded by ten smaller ones. "I'd like to have that as my Hajdú cape."

"Don't touch." His mother grabs his hand.

"I'd wear those stars on my Hajdú hat," Gabi says. "Look at them glow." Tomi's gaze follows the beam illuminating the stars. It's coming from the stained-glass yarmulke. "I wish I had my slingshot," Gabi says quietly as he nudges Tomi.

"What are those?" Tomi asks, pointing at the different-sized golden pipes sticking out from behind the ark.

"Golden whistles."

"They're organ pipes," Emma-mama says. "They're attached to an organ, which is like a piano but it has a lot more keys and pedals. I love organ music. When I was young, on Sundays, I used to sit on the church steps and listen. It sounded like a hundred cantors."

"Why didn't you go inside?"

"Churches are for Christians. We weren't allowed in."

"Because we killed Jesus?"

"Where did you hear that?"

"Carrot told us."

"We didn't kill Jesus," his mother snapped. "Jews don't kill Jews."

"Jesus was Jewish? When did he become a Christian?"

"He didn't. He was always Jewish."

Tomi is confused. So is everybody Jewish?"

"No," his mother answers.

"So why couldn't you go in the church?" Gabi asks.

"Because we were Jews."

"Was there an organ in our synagogue?"

"Synagogues don't have organs."

"So why does this synagogue have one?"

"I don't know."

"What's a Garden of Remembrance?" Tomi asks pointing to a door.

Emma-mama hesitates. "I don't know, maybe a garden to remember things in. Maybe they have roses."

"Let's go," Gabi says.

"No," his mother cries, but Gabi has already pushed open the door.

"It's beautiful." Emma-mama smiles. "Like a palace garden."

An arcade with pillared arches runs along three sides. In the middle large weeping willows are surrounded by granite plaques. They stand like sad grey guards. "Even in the winter they are beautiful." Emma-mama points to the one in the centre of the courtyard.

"Look." Tomi points to plaques that lie flat around the tree. He kneels. "They have names and dates on them. Are there dead people in here?"

When he turns around, he sees his mother and Emma-mama holding each other. "Why are you crying?"

"What's the matter?" Gabi asks.

Emma-mama kneels and hugs Gabi tightly and continues crying. Tomi's mother grips his hand and stares at the plaques. She is also crying. "Let's go back," she says.

"Who are they?" Gabi asks.

"Family," Emma-mama says very quietly as they turn to leave.

——

How could all those people be family? he wants to ask, but he senses this is not the time. His mother and Emma-mama sit with their eyes closed, heads down, holding hands. Gabi is sleeping with his head on his mother's lap.

"Read from the book, please," Tomi says to his mother when she finally opens her eyes. She likes reading to him. Maybe it will bring her smile back.

"Okay," she says softly. "Get me the book." Tomi fishes it out and shows his mother where he left off. It was at the most exciting part, close to the end. Lying in bed, sick and delirious from being dunked into the icy lake, Nemecsek is still determined to be part of the fight.

He leans into her as she begins to read. The defence of the fort was going badly for the Paul Street boys. They were being overwhelmed and only a few remained standing. Feri, leader of the Red Shirts, was about to climb to the tower to capture their flag. If he did, then the Paul Street boys would be defeated and their fort would be handed over to the Red Shirts.

Feri Áts, charging furiously, ran ahead; the hope of victory was in his voice. "After me!"

But he suddenly stopped, for at that very moment something seemed to roll up to his feet. A frail childish figure sprang at him from beside the shack. The red-shirt chief was taken aback and the fierce warriors behind him piled up against him with a jolt.

The little boy stood before Feri Áts, a lad fully a head smaller than himself. The thin blond boy raised his hands in protest. His childish voice cried out: "Halt!"

The Paul Street army, which had been somewhat dismayed by the sudden turn of affairs, now burst into a spontaneous "Nemecsek!"

And the sandy little slim child suddenly picked up big Feri Áts and—with a superhuman effort, born of his feverish temperature and semi-delirium—hurled the surprised leader to the ground in real style.

Then he too collapsed, swooning atop the sprawling body of his victim.

Tomi's mother closes the book.

"Can you read some more now? Please?"

"No, then there won't be anything to read later," she says, handing him back the book. "Now be a good little boy, like the child in Attila's poem, and lie down and rest."

"I'm not a little boy," he says, but he lies down, his head on his mother's lap. He wraps his arms around his book. He knows how the story ends, but still, he always feels sad.

"They've been gone over an hour," Emma says. "Where are they?"

"I don't know, but don't worry. Sanyi has a way of getting side-tracked."

His mother tries not to sound worried but Tomi feels that she is. He is beginning to sense that grownups don't always mean what they say. Sometimes they pretend to be one way but are another. Sometimes they smile when they are sad and sometimes they lie. Nemecsek never lied. Tomi drifts off thinking about Frog, wondering what he's up to.

"I'm hungry," Gabi says, yawning. "Aren't you?" he asks Tomi, who is also waking up and stretching. He is, but he doesn't want to bother his mother.

"No."

"Papa hasn't come back yet. We'll eat when they return," Emma-mama says.

"Can we explore some more?" Tomi asks. "We promise to behave." He rubs his arm for sympathy.

"As long as you're back soon."

"And don't go outside."

The boys snake in and out of the pews all the way to the front of the synagogue.

"Look! A museum!" Gabi points to a sign across from the Garden of Remembrance. "Let's go!"

Tomi follows him up three flights of marble stairs. "Maybe there'll be swords and shields."

"And helmets and armour!"

They enter an all-white room made even whiter by the light streaming in through the big windows. But there are no swords, shields or armour. Instead, there are rows of glass cabinets containing shiny metal cups, old books with gold writing, scrolls, and shiny silver Ten Commandments that Tomi knows are laid over the Torah, like a breastplate.

"What's that?" Tomi asks, pointing to what looks like a small shiny bird cage.

Gabi reads the card beside it. "Censer. From the Ottoman Empire period, 1530."

"They were the evil Turks."

Gabi nods. "It's old."

"What's a censer?" asked Tomi.

"Who knows? This place is boring. It's just some old stuff from synagogues. Where are the swords and shields?"

"Maybe they're in there." Tomi points to a doorway at the far end.

They hesitate at the entrance. The room is dark. Gabi takes Tomi's hand as they make their way inside.

"Maybe it's a dungeon," Tomi says

"They don't have dungeons in synagogues. And besides, dungeons are in basements."

"It feels like a dungeon."

"How would you know? You've never been in one."

"Don't you remember *The Count of Monte Cristo?* Your mother read it to us. Those dungeons had walls just like these."

There are no windows.

"All the place needs is rotting hay on the floor, a few rats running around and a couple of bearded, long-haired, smelly prisoners chained to the walls."

"And torture stuff like the rack."

There are no knightly weapons or armour here, either. Only more glass cases. One has a dress in it. A note beside it explains that the dress was made from prayer shawls.

"This drumhead was made from a de-se-cra-ted Torah."

"What does de-se-cra-ted mean?" he asks

Gabi shrugs his shoulders. "Maybe it's a special Torah."

"Remember Rabbi Stern telling us that Torahs a long, long, long time ago were made of animal skins? Maybe desecrated was a special kind of animal that doesn't exist anymore, like a dinosaur," says Tomi.

"Don't be stupid. There is no animal called desecrated."

"How do you know?"

"I'm older," Gabi says and turns to look at the pictures on the walls.

The old photographs are of bearded men like Rabbi Stern, and young men and women who look just like his parents, some holding babies and children about the same ages as them. All of them have stars on their clothes. They don't look happy or sad, just blank. They make him afraid. He can hear his own heartbeat and his breathing.

"It looks like these pictures were taken in this synagogue."

"Gabi, why are they wearing the Star of David?"

Gabi shrugs and reads the inscription: "Budapest Ghetto Jews."

"What's a ghetto?" Tomi asks.

"How should I know?" He reads from another. "This picture is from The Garden of Remembrance."

"It's filled with bodies piled on top of one another."

Looking down on the piles are serious men in long coats with armbands that have arrows on them. Gabi continues reading. "The Jewish victims of Arrow Cross men in the court of Dohány Street Synagogue, 1944."

"What are the Arrow Cross men?"

"I don't know. Maybe they're hunters who use bows and arrows to hunt." Gabi takes hold of Tomi's hand again.

He can't stop staring. He learned about the war in school. It was all about heroic Russians and Hungarians, not Jews. Those bodies piled on top of each other don't look like brave soldiers who died noble or heroic deaths. Who were the Arrow Cross men and why were they standing guard over them? Were they protecting them? He didn't think so. Maybe they died because they killed Jesus? But his mother had told him that the Jews didn't kill Jesus. So why? He's filled with questions. And every time he thinks of one, another pops into his head. What happened to those relatives of his? Why do these photographs make him feel sad and angry?

———

"Where were you boys?" Emma-mama asks. "We were starting to worry."

"There's a museum upstairs that has all sorts of old books and goblets and pictures."

"That's nice," she says.

"Papa!"

"What took you so long?" His mother sounds both upset and relieved.

"Most of the stores were shut or looted. We had to do some back-door knocking."

"And?" Emma-mama asks.

They reached into their briefcases and produced half a loaf of rye bread and a quarter salami rod. "Kosher," his father says.

"And…" Dezsö reaches into his bag, pulls out a shiny apple and hands it to Gabi's mother.

"Ohhh," she sighs.

But no rock candy. Though disappointed, Tomi doesn't let it show. It isn't that important, he tells himself.

"What's going on outside?" his mother asks.

"It's not looking good," Dezsö-papa answers. "There are a lot of people running around and some gunfire."

"Are the Russians back?"

His father nods. "That's what everybody's saying."

His mother starts to lay out the food. She hands everyone a piece of bread, and two slices of salami. Tomi is about to bite into his bread when his father reaches out and stops him. His father begins to recite in Yiddish.

"It's the prayer for bread," Gabi whispers.

"I know." He knows the words but doesn't know what they all mean. He knows "lechem" means bread and "Elohaynu" means God.

"Amen," they all repeat. Even Dezsö-papa.

Tomi is used to his grandfather's constant praying. He prays when he wakes up, when he washes his hands, before eating, before going to bed. He even prays after going to the bathroom! But not his father. And now, twice in two days.

"Why do you pray?"

"Because we thank God for the bread."

"But it's the baker who makes the bread. Is he God?"

"Yes, the baker makes the bread, but God made the wheat from which the baker made the bread."

"Who made God?"

"That's a good one, Sanyi." Dezsö-papa is smiling.

"Why did our relatives have to wear the Star of David during the war?"

"Where did you get that idea from, Gabi?" Emma-mama asks.

"We saw pictures of people in the museum and they were in The Garden of Remembrance and they were wearing Stars of David."

Nobody answers. Then Dezsö-papa says, "To show that they were special."

Sanyi looks at Dezsö and nods.

There are so many questions Tomi wants to ask but the silence tells him that this isn't the right time. He wonders how you know when it's the right time. The parents look very serious, like they're thinking of something grown-up, something important. His parents look like the people in the photographs. He starts to cry.

"What's the matter?" his mother asks. "Is your face hurting? Is your arm okay?" She looks worried. "Let me see."

"It's okay. It's okay. It's not going to hurt," his mother consoles him as she unbuttons his shirt. Gently and slowly, she pulls his arm from the sleeve, unties the bandage and tugs at the gauze.

Tomi cries out.

"It's okay. It won't hurt," she said, ripping it off without any warning.

"That hurt!"

"It's done." She blows gently over the iodine-coloured area. "See? It looks better already."

Gabi studies Tomi's face. "Is he going to have a scar?" he asks.

"Of course not! Don't even think about it." Emma-mama snaps. "Where do you get such a silly idea?"

"Too bad. Scars make you look like a real hero."

"I'm going to put some more iodine and a new piece of gauze to make sure it doesn't get infected. Okay?"

Tomi tries to pull his arm out of his mother's grip. "It's going to hurt, I know it will!"

"It'll sting a little, but you're a brave soldier, aren't you?"

"Like Nemecsek," Gabi says.

"Yes."

"Now close your eyes and take a deep breath."

He closes his eyes, clenches his jaw and hisses through his teeth while his mother dabs iodine on the wounds. She blows softly over the cuts.

"Okay. All done. You can open your eyes now."

When he opens his eyes, he sees his father standing in front of him, holding out a little brown bag.

"Happy birthday."

What? Is it really his birthday? He had completely forgotten. It is just like his father promised, they are in Budapest for his birthday.

"What is it?" he asks as he reaches for the bag.

"Guess."

"Rock candy!" Gabi shouts.

"Really?"

"Thank you. Thank you!" He hugs his father, then his mother. He can't stop smiling. "Thank you!"

He looks inside the bag. He can't believe his eyes—little rocks of every shape and size, some milky, some shiny, some sharp and pointy, each of them a beautiful gem.

"Well? Are you going spend all day staring at them or are you going to eat one?" his father asks.

Tomi sits next to Gabi. "Here. Choose."

—

Tomi is asleep, his head in Hannah's lap. She is gently stroking his brow, feeling the little pock marks where the slivers struck. Thank God none had gotten in his eyes. Thank God for Mrs. Aranyi. She made Hannah realize how much she missed her own mother, how much a child needs her mother. She can't believe it. Tomi is eight, already eight! God, how time flies. But he's still just a child. He shouldn't be going through these things. This is why she didn't want children. It's not fair. God, it's not fair. He shouldn't have to deal with hate and war. God, isn't it enough that we went through it? Wasn't Faigele eight…?

A loud Amen and the huge chandeliers exploding into light startles Hannah. Her sudden movement wakes Tomi. Looking up from his mother's lap into the brightness forces him to shield his eyes. He's not sure where he is. Then he remembers. Sitting up, he sees something at the front of the synagogue that wasn't there before, what look like statues draped in white cloth. They're moving, rocking back and forth. The statues turn toward him. They remove the cloths from their heads. One of them is his father. He and the others start walking towards them. They look like they're wearing capes, capes that have the same pattern as the dress he saw in the museum. As his father gets nearer, Tomi sees that his collar is covered in shiny silvery little squares, like chain mail. Striding toward him with his cape billowing, his father looks like a noble lord from long, long, long ago.

"What's he wearing?"

"That's his prayer shawl. Every Jewish boy gets one when he turns thirteen; that's when a Jewish boy becomes a man."

"I thought that I became a man when I drank the pálinka."

"Yes, but for us, it's different. It's when you are thirteen that you become an adult member of the tribe."

"We belong to a tribe? Like Indians?"

"No, of course not. We're Jewish. Your father and you belong to the noble tribe of Cohens."

"Do we fight like the Hajdús?"

"Not now, but yes, a long time ago they did. But the Cohens are extra special because they are also the priest tribe."

"What did I do to become a Cohen?"

"You have to be born into it."

"Like kings can only be from other kings?"

"Yes."

"Hey," he calls to Gabi, who is also just waking up, "I'm a rabbi warrior!"

"No, you're not. You don't have a beard."

"The Sabbath is over," his father says as he takes off his thalith, folds it carefully, brings it to his lips and carefully places it in its blue cloth case. He kisses Tomi's mother on her forehead and pats Tomi. "Time to go."

Everyone is making their way out. People are wishing each other "Good Sabbath" and "Next year in Israel." Tomi tugs on his father's arm. "I want to kiss the mezuzah. I'm a Cohen."

15

It's dark outside, darker than the night before. Fewer street lamps seem to be lit. Not many people are out tonight, and those who are seem to be in a serious hurry to get somewhere. Those leaving the synagogue stick close to the walls of buildings, trying to be as invisible as possible. But with everyone heading in the same direction, most with luggage, they look like a herd. Dezsö-papa starts to follow them.

"No, this way," his father says, turning into an alley. "This way's quicker."

The alley is even darker than the street. The only sound is their click-clacking shoes on the cobblestones. His father leads them, zig-zagging from alley to alley, until at last they come out onto a small square with one lamppost in the middle of it. There's a group of people chanting, "Yes. Yes. Yes."

His mother and Emma-mama hold hands. Gabi and he are scooped up by their fathers. From his perch, Tomi can make out a rope tied around the neck of the lamppost. He thinks that they're trying to topple it like the statue in Békes. The rope is swaying back and forth. Something is hanging from it. The shouts seem to get louder and sound angrier as they approach the crowd. His father stops at the edge of the gathering. He turns quickly to go around it rather than through it. A few people turn to look at them but then turn back to what is happening in the middle.

Tomi cranes his head to get a better view. The thing hanging from the rope, that he thought was a bag, is a man upside down! His arms are tied to his waist. His shirt is torn off. The light shines on his pale skin that has lots of small dark spots. There is money sticking out of his mouth. Tomi wants to look away from the scene, but he can't. It's directly in his view. People are screaming "Rotten AVO!" while others spit on the man and jab him with their burning cigarettes. They're chanting "Yes. Yes. Yes," as men take turns kicking his head as though it's a soccer ball.

"Oh, my God! Oh, my God!" Emma-mama is holding her mouth like she is going to be sick.

Tomi screams but no sound comes out of his mouth. His father's hand is pressing hard against his face but through his father's spread fingers he can still see the swaying body and the kicking.

———

"We're here," his father says.

Kids with slingshots are running around shooting out street-lamp bulbs. The entrance to the train station is barricaded now by a semi-circle of overturned trucks and streetcars. Men and women are positioned behind the barricades, rifles and machine guns at the ready. They look like the same people he saw last night happily strolling the streets, except tonight nobody is smiling.

The two families hurry into the station. It's also dark, the few lights and the steam and smoke rising from the engines making it look more like a cave full of shadows and evil than a crystal train palace.

Although his father's shortcut got them to the station ahead of most people, the cars are already filling up. People jostle each other to get on board. The conductors' lanterns, swinging back and forth sending messages to the engineers, remind Tomi of the body he just saw swinging back and forth like the pendulum of his grandfather's clock.

The sound of gunfire and the rumbling of tanks grows louder and nearer.

"When are we leaving?" Emma asks, staring out the window.

"Soon," Dezső-papa reassures her. "Soon."

"Why were they kicking that man?" Tomi asks once they are settled into their seats.

"Because he was a bad man," his father says.

"Why did he have money in his mouth?"

"Because he stole from the people."

Tomi doesn't understand.

The rotten pig!" Dezsö-papa spits.

"Why was he a rotten pig?" Gabi asks. He looks scared.

"He deserved it."

"Dezsö! Enough!"

"He was an AVO. The AVOs are animals who come at night, break down your door and take you away. It doesn't matter whether you are guilty or innocent. To them you are guilty. Period. They starve you and they beat you."

"Why?" Gabi asks.

"Dezsö! Enough! Haven't they seen enough?" Emma-mama yells. Tomi has never seen Emma-mama that angry. She looks like she is ready to claw him. Everybody in the car looks at them. Dezsö stares long and hard at her and looks like he's going to scream back at her.

Tomi points to the front of the car. "Look! It's the Baroness."

Mrs. Darvas, still wearing her two coats, is shoving her way down the aisle. She looks angry.

"See? We're late because of you. Find us a seat!" she is shouting at Mr. Darvas who is following behind, huffing and puffing, carrying the same two heavy suitcases. There are no empty seats. She stops beside them.

Mr. Darvas sets down the suitcases and gestures for her to sit on one. She looks at the luggage, then at him. She angrily shakes her head. She looks at her husband the way Mrs. Gombás would look at students when they said or did something stupid. She turns toward Tomi's mother, who stares back. Mrs. Darvas looks away.

"Ágnes, why don't you sit down here? Tomi, sit on Mama's lap," Sanyi says. Mrs. Darvas clenches her jaw and looks like she is ready to spit. Hannah gives Sanyi a hard look as she reaches over and lifts Tomi onto her lap. His father slides over as Mrs. Darvas sits down with a thump that sends Sanyi bumping into his mother.

Dezsö-papa helps Mr. Darvas lift the suitcases onto the racks above them.

"Thanks." Mr. Darvas sighs, wiping the sweat off the back of his neck. Lifting Gabi onto her lap, Emma-mama makes room for him.

"All aboard!" the conductor shouts and blows his whistle. Tomi presses his face against the window and watches the conductor on the platform waving his lantern back and forth.

"How long before we get to Israel?"

"First we have to get to Sopron," his mother says.

"All aboard the Freedom Express!" the conductor shouts as the train lurches before starting on its way.

As the train slides out of the station into the open night, Tomi looks back. The glass palace is getting smaller and smaller. The flickering lights of the city disappear. Loud claps of thunder fill the air. He can't tell whether the sound is coming from the sky or the tanks.

On his birthday, he was wounded. He saw a soldier shot and a tank blown up by kids. He found out that he belonged to an important tribe. He was in a synagogue as big and as beautiful as a palace. He saw a cemetery filled with relatives he didn't know about. He saw pictures of bodies piled up on top of each other. He saw people kicking a person who was hanging upside down. He saw people hiding and aiming guns from behind overturned trucks and streetcars. And now he was on a train to Israel.

He wants to ask his parents so many questions. He wants to know the meaning of big words like de-se-cra-tion. He wants to know what a ghetto is, and what people concentrated on while they were in a concentration camp. But something tells him he isn't supposed to be asking these questions now. Maybe that's what it means to be a grown-up; not the drinking of pálinka or being thirteen, but knowing when to ask questions and when not to.

He reaches into his pocket and feels the familiar edges of his rock candy and the handle of his penknife. He leans into his mother and drifts off to sleep.

"Look, Tomi! There's the Golden Green!" Sanyi says, but his son is asleep.

Sanyi strokes the boy's forehead, arches his hands over him and quietly recites, "May God bless you and watch over you. May God shine His face toward you and show you favour. May God grant you peace." Those around him who are still awake murmur "Amen." Even Ágnes.

Hannah smiles at Sanyi and mouths "Amen." She leans her forehead into the cold window and closes her eyes too.

16

She didn't really know how long they'd been travelling. Maybe two, maybe three days and nights. There was no routine to judge by. The train stopped at all hours for hours, in the dark, in the daytime. Sometimes the doors were opened, other times not. Packed in the way they were made her constantly feel short of breath. The air reeked of excrement and vomit. They were forced to relieve themselves through the gaps in the floor. She didn't know where they were going. That was a big part of the fear. Nobody knew. What she did know was that wherever it was, it was not good.

She also knew the why. That answer was as old as the Jews. But why the Jews she didn't know. And although the Jews and gentiles of Szabad co-existed side by side, there was always the difference. They lived among the gentiles, but they were never of them. They were friendly, but they were never friends. All Hannah's friends were Jewish and they were here in the cattle cars with her.

The young and healthy stood in the unbearable heat while the old and sick lay on the floor moaning, crying, praying, dying.

Families huddled and held onto each other. Hannah, Magda and their mother formed a circle around Faigele. They tried to protect her from the constant push and shove of others. Hannah felt nauseous but the thought of throwing up kept her from doing it.

Whenever the train stopped the guards opened the doors and ordered the prisoners to throw off the corpses. The living were sometimes given what looked and smelled like the slop farmers fed their pigs. It tasted like cold dishwater. The guards tossed in slices of bread and howled with laughter at the spectacle of women screaming, scrambling, pushing and shoving each other for the mouldy slices.

Although they were country girls who liked to eat well, Hannah and Magda were accustomed to not eating for long stretches of time. Ever since the war had begun food was hard to come by and eating frugally was what everyone did.

"Save some for later," Hannah's mother instructed them as she pinched a few morsels to eat and put away the rest in her pocket. Hannah and Magda did the same. Being only eight, Faigele was allowed to eat half of her slice.

——

It was still dark when the train lurched to a halt. The prisoners slammed into one another, into walls, fell on top of the dead and dying bodies. People screamed from pain, from fear.

The doors slid open. The women stood, dazed, trying to adjust to the dark. A sudden explosion of lights blinded them. Voices from behind the lights bellowed at them in Yiddish and Hungarian. "Get off. Get off. Leave your belongings behind. Hurry up, hurry up, or they'll beat you."

Ghostlike figures in striped pyjamas emerged from the dark. "Quick! Quick!" they kept yelling, their dead eyes focused on nothing. They climbed aboard the train and tossed out the luggage and the dead.

Soldiers with German shepherds straining on leashes marched along the platform shouting at everyone to get into line. Officers with skulls on their hats and collars and riding crops in their hands stood at the ready, while Hannah and the rest of the new arrivals shivered in the November chill.

Marching music started blaring as morning broke. Barking dogs and shouting guards added to the cacophony. The smell of fear was almost visible. In the growing daylight Hannah could make out row after grey row of long wooden buildings, from which emaciated men and women in prison pyjamas emerged and formed lines. She could see barbed-wire fences and towers, from where guards aimed their rifles at them.

She held tightly onto Magda's hand. The entire camp stood still and quiet. Then a shrill whistle broke the silence and the lines shuffled off in different directions. The spotlights snapped off. Through the misty vapours other ghosts appeared with wheelbarrows to collect the luggage and the dead. She looked at them. No one looked back.

"Move!" barked a gruff voice in German. The ghosts repeated the order in Yiddish and Hungarian. "Hands by your side!"

The women and children were marched across the yard to a long table, where officers shuffling lists sat on either side of a man in a white doctor's coat. Some of them were women. They were the first women soldiers she had ever seen. Hannah felt relief.

The doctor looked them up and down, the way a butcher inspects a slab of meat. He looked at Hannah's mother and then at Faigele.

"Age?" one the officers barked at Faigele.

Faigele clutched her mother's hand.

"Age," one of the women soldiers shouted. Faigele began to cry again.

The doctor wrinkled his brow and waved the officer off with his hand. Then he turned and smiled at Faigele. His voice was gentle. "My name is Doctor Mengele. What's your name?" Another of the sullen, dead-eyed ghosts translated his words for her.

"Faigele," she said.

"And how old are you, Faigele?" he asked.

"Eight."

"Good," he smiled. "Now please go stand over there with your mother." He pointed to his right.

When it was their turn, Hannah and Magda also were sent to the right. The officers finished going through the list, and then all those on the right were marched into a windowless brick building and given a threadbare towel and a bar of soap.

"Undress! Quick!" the ghosts repeated the guards' orders. "Towels on the hooks. Remember your hook number."

Grandmothers, mothers, wives and young girls who had never been naked before any one, not even their husbands, cried out in protest but were quickly beaten back into silence. They shuffled to get away from the slaps and in the momentary chaos, Magda grabbed the gold links from their clothes.

"No crying now," the woman in charge said. "You're dirty from the long trip. You're just going to clean yourselves. Now go into the shower room," she said in a gentle voice, "so you will become clean pure Jews."

When the last woman was in, the door was bolted shut. Hannah jumped at the sound. Magda held her hand tight. The room was silent as the women waited for the shower to start. Hannah looked around and marvelled at the rows and rows of showerheads in the ceiling. She had heard of showers but she had never taken one. Hannah had heard that sometimes hot water came out of them. Hot water. They didn't even have cold running water at home. She lifted her head up, closed her eyes and waited for that mysterious warm stream of water to cleanse her.

The door banged open. An officer and a guard strode in. The panicked women began screaming and tried to cover themselves. The guard stood at the door while the officer marched about, pointing to several of the women, Hannah and Magda included.

"Out," he shouted.

"Hurry up! Hurry up!" the guard yelled at them.

"I want to stay with Mama!" Hannah cried. The guard gave her a vicious shove. "Move!"

Magda took her hand and led her out. They soon found themselves marching toward another building where another group of ghosts stood behind rows of chairs, ready with scissors and clippers.

"Don't cry. Don't be afraid," Magda whispered.

Hannah was proud of her thick, shiny black hair. Her mother had always taken care to keep their hair free of lice. They washed it once a week before the Sabbath. It was a ritual Hannah loved. Her mother washed each girl's hair with a special homemade soap in which she put lavender from her garden. Then she made them sit in a row on the kitchen bench and brush each other's hair: Her mother brushed Magda's, who brushed Hannah's, who brushed Faigele's. She always felt so pretty after her weekly hair wash.

Tears streaked down her cheeks as her beautiful hair fell to the ground. She felt more naked than when she had been forced to undress in front of the guards. Once everyone was shaved, they were ordered into a large empty room, where they were sprayed with a white powder that made her cough, then into another room where they were given prison clothes. They dressed wordlessly, and were marched out to wait. Hannah felt ugly.

She began to gag. Terrified, she tried to keep from vomiting, but her deep, convulsive breaths only made matters worse. She clamped her hands over her mouth to push down whatever was about to come up. The stench was vile. It was coming from the high chimney next to the shower building. "Mama! Faigele!" Hannah cried out.

17

The train screeches to a halt. Tomi lurches awake and sees an old man tumbling down the aisle. The man lands in Mrs. Darvas's lap.

"Get him off me! Get him off me!" she shrieks and shoves him into her husband, knocking him back against his seat. His feet shoot out, kicking Mrs. Darvas in the shins, who screams and kicks back. Her husband curses and shoves the old man back toward Mrs. Darvas. Tomi's father and Dezsö-papa leap up and grab the old man, who is calling out to God. They help him to his feet. As he lunges Tomi's father accidently hits Mrs. Darvas in the mouth, knocking her into shocked silence.

Everyone is shouting at once. Tomi's mother looks out the window. "What's going on? Where are we? Why are we stopping? There's no station here."

"Sopron is still an hour away," his father says looking at his watch. The worry in his parents' voices and the way his mother holds him so tightly scares him.

"Maybe there's something on the tracks," Dezsö-papa says.

"Find out why we stopped," Mrs. Darvas yells at her husband, who is still rubbing his shins.

Before he can answer, the doors of the train car bang open. Uniformed men with rifles appear at each end of the car. An immediate silence falls over the passengers. The uniformed men stomp to attention as two men in leather coats and fedoras board the car. Their hats cast shadows over their faces.

"Everybody stay where you are! Don't move! No talking!" the shorter of the two shouts. "Prepare to show your Identity Books!"

"It's the bloody AVO," Dezső-papa whispers under his breath.

"Oh, my God! No! God damn them!" Emma-mama's face goes white. She looks scared and angry at the same time. She wraps her arms around Gabi and balls her hands into fists.

Gabi's father puts his palm to her lips.

"I don't want them near me!"

Tomi keeps trying to see their faces. Dezső-papa's words race through his mind: "Faceless animals who come at night, break down your door and take you away. They're animals. They beat you. They starve you." He leans further into his mother.

"Didn't you hear us? Silence!" shouts the other one. They advance through the car, shouting at people to show their Identity Books. They start ordering some off the train.

"Papers!" the shorter man keeps shouting.

They aren't animals. They have normal people faces but with mean eyes and mouths. The taller one turns to Mr. Darvas, while the shorter questions his father.

Tomi watches their every move. Mr. Darvas hands over an envelope while his father hands their books to the other man. The taller one looks in the envelope, takes out the books, puts the envelope in his pocket and hands back the books without looking at them. The shorter one looks at every page of their books slowly. He looks at them and then at their books and back at his parents again, as if he is waiting for something.

"You three. Off! Now!"

His mother puts her arms around his waist and tightens her grip.

"Didn't you hear me?" The shorter man grabs his mother by the arm and jerks her hard. "I said off!"

"Don't hurt my mother!" Tomi grabs the AVO's hand. He feels a smack on his face, snapping his head into his mother's chin. They both cry out in pain.

"Don't touch them!" his father jumps between them and the AVO man.

"You! Shut up and move!"

His father reaches for Tomi, who is crying and holding his face, and lifts him up. His mother is reluctant to let go. "Don't cry," his father whispers, wiping away the blood from his nose. "It's going to be all right," his father says and steps into the aisle. Hannah, holding her chin, follows.

"You three, also!" barks the taller officer at Gabi's parents.

"No!" Dezsö-papa shouts. He lunges forward and punches the AVO man in the face. "No! No! You God-damned pigs," he shouts as he swings at the shorter AVO man. The punch sends the second man flying into passengers standing in the aisle, who try to shove him away from them if he were some sort of insect. The other, whose nose is bleeding, tries to grab Dezsö-papa, but can't pin his swinging arms.

"No. Oh, my God! No!" Tomi sees Emma-mama screaming, putting herself between Gabi and the men. People are shoving each other, trying to protect themselves and their families, trying to stay out of the way. They're slipping and falling on top of each other. They're trying to grab their suitcases, causing others to fall from the overhead compartment and hit people on their heads. The guards at each end of the car start butt-ending, pushing, elbowing their way, yelling at people to clear the way, but they can't get through. Trapped in the crush, Tomi feels his breath being squeezed out him.

"Mama!" Tomi shouts, seeing his mother being dragged backwards. His father grabs her by her collar and tugs hard, but she's stuck. He tries again, but only manages to tear it. "Mama!" Tomi yells again and reaches out and grabs her by her hair. She screams but this gives his father a chance to grab her by her arm and pull. He pulls her through. With Tomi in one arm, and his wife by the arm, like a bull, he snorts, grunts and shoves his way through the crowd. He manages to get to the end of the car, where he throws open the toilet door, yanks his wife in with him, and quickly shuts the door.

It's dark inside. Suddenly Tomi's very scared. "Let me out! Let me out! I want to get out," he yells.

He feels his father's strong hand over his mouth. "Be quiet!"
Tomi freezes.

"Hannah, hold him and make sure he stays quiet."

His mother takes him and sets him down on the toilet seat.
"Stay there!" Tomi's arm and face hurt, but he's afraid to cry out.
His father leans against the door. He hears yelling, cursing and
pleading. He's trembling. He wants to know what's happening
to Gabi, Emma-mama and Dezső-papa. A hard thud against the
door throws the door open and his father backwards. His mother
rushes to help. She leans her back against the door. His father
bolts it. Tomi jumps off the toilet and puts both his hands against
the door. Together, they lean and wait.

"Never again. Never again. Never again," he hears his mother
saying under her breath. She sounds like she's praying.

"Shhh!" his father snaps. "Do you want them to find us?"

"Never again," she hisses and grabs Tomi tightly.

"You're hurting me!"

His father clamps his hand over Tomi's mouth and nose.
Tomi tries to pry his father's hand loose but can't. Gasping for air,
he kicks his father in the shin.

His father grunts, letting go.

"I couldn't breathe," Tomi gasps and leans into the door.
There is more yelling and shouting and struggling. He wants to
cry. "I won't cry. I won't cry," he repeats to himself. He can hear his
parents' and his own loud breathing. The noises outside the door
recede.

The whistle blows, startling him. But before any sound comes
out, he claps his hand over his mouth. The train jerks backwards
and forwards. He lands on the toilet seat. The train starts moving
again.

His father taps his mother on the shoulder and signals her to
sit. He reaches out and gently lifts Tomi onto her lap. He kisses the
top of his head, takes off his leather coat, and spreads it over them
like a blanket. Tomi's mother takes out her handkerchief and wipes
his nose. "Are you okay?" she asks quietly as she strokes his face.

"It hurts but not much," he whispers as she touches the swelling on his cheek.

"Oh, my baby, my baby. Those rotten lice!"

He can't tell which way they're moving, back home to Békes or to Israel. He hopes they're going home.

"Try to get some sleep, Hannah," his father whispers.

"Not until we're out of this damned country." His mother caresses Tomi's head, repeating with each stroke, "Never again."

Curled up on his mother's lap, her warm breath on the back of his neck, he feels safe.

The place stinks.

18

Hannah remembers being transferred from Auschwitz to the Niemen's Cable Factory to be a slave worker. She hadn't wanted to leave the camp, hadn't wanted to leave Magda. Her mother and her little sister Faigele had been gassed and cremated here. They had become the smoke here, the ash, the barren earth she walked upon. In truth, she would just as soon die here herself. But she had no say in her own life. Being a slave meant being stripped of any power over your fate. You belonged to these animals. They emptied you of life. You became a thing, nothing more than a tool to be used until you broke. And then you were thrown away. What was the point of living?

Magda was having none of it. "As long as you're alive, you fight," her sister told her. "You don't give up. You make these animals work for that."

Magda traded one of the gold chain links to get herself transferred to the Niemen's Cable Factory too. Most tried to avoid it, but Magda volunteered herself and Hannah for the hardest labour at the cable company, the job of rolling large spools of copper wire from the yard into the factory. She traded their volunteering with the other slaves for extra food and tobacco. The tobacco she gave to the guard to ensure that they stayed together.

Hannah remembers standing in the early mornings, next to Magda, waiting to be counted. Staring straight ahead as the guards walked between the rows, hitting anyone who didn't answer fast enough. And never seeing again those who fell and couldn't get back up. This was her daily life. This was normal.

Hannah remembers lining up after roll call for watery porridge, cold watered-down chicory coffee and a slice of mouldy bread. Being the oldest living one, Magda was now the mama, and was always nagging Hannah to save as much of her bread as she could, constantly reminding her, "Bread is money."

Hannah remembers the daily labour and the daily labour of survival; the numbness. She stopped feeling. She lost track of time. Days, weeks, months, years lost all meaning. And she didn't care. She knew she was in hell and she wasn't getting out. Barely alive among the barely living, she was becoming one of the shadowless ghosts she had seen when she first arrived. But Magda wouldn't let her. Magda pushed her on and fed her, if not hope, a desire for revenge.

Yes, Hannah remembers.

—

When it first began, it was a faint drone. The normal sound of machinery. But when it began to sound more like a swarm of mosquitoes, she knew. Everybody knew. They looked up and saw the airplanes. Earlier during the war the planes had been German but more and more often these past weeks, they were Allied bombers. Stars instead of iron crosses were flying overhead. And now they were flying daytime missions, bombing factories.

Anichka, a Czechoslovakian woman with whom Magda traded, told them daytime flights meant that the Germans were losing the war. "The end is near," the women whispered to each other at night as they lay exhausted on their hard cots before sleep. They had said this before, but then it was out of hopelessness. Now it was with hope. But it also gave rise to fear. Bombs didn't differentiate between prisoners and guards, between Nazis and Jews. "Freedom and death falling from the sky. Life and death at the same time." Anichka said one night, "Who would have thought that we would have to fear both the Nazis and the Americans?"

That day, when the sirens sounded, the guards ran into their bomb shelters, while the slaves tried to find cover in the factory.

Instead of following the others, Magda grabbed Hannah by the wrist and said, "Come on!"

"What are you doing? It's safer inside."

Behind the building, Magda peeled back a section of the fence. Soon she was on the ground and crawling through the hole like a worm.

"What are you doing?"

"Come, quick!" Magda urged as she held the wire for Hannah to crawl through. As loud explosions rocked the air, they began to run.

The earth blew up. Hannah was flying through the air; forever, it seemed. Pellets of earth shot into her ears, eyes and mouth. She went blind. She gagged. Finally her body was slammed into the ground and she lay there, breathless, unable to move.

She was inside a loud buzzing. It was getting louder and picking up speed. I'm going to explode, she thought. She gritted her teeth and waited. Maybe this is the sound of death. Maybe this is death, a forever buzzing. She felt a touch. She jerked. The touch became two claws grasping her shoulders. She was being shaken. She tried to raise her head but she couldn't. The dead don't get up, she thought. Her neck hurt. Do the dead hurt? Do they talk to themselves? She felt herself being pulled to her feet. She opened her eyes. They hurt from the grit. She blinked and rubbed her eyes. Magda stood in front of her. Her sister's lips were moving but there was no sound.

Hannah leaned closer. Magda's lips were moving again, but this time more slowly.

"What?" she shouted, startling Magda, who jumped backwards but quickly recovered to clamp a hand over Hannah's mouth.

Magda's lips looked like fish lips, moving but saying nothing. Hannah pointed to her ear. Magda's lips kept moving. She pointed to her mouth and then to Hannah's ear. Hannah nodded. A spasm of pain shot through her neck. She cried out but didn't hear herself. She grabbed her neck and pressed, but the buzz continued relentlessly.

"No," she said but couldn't hear herself.

Magda stood watching her helplessly. Then she took Hannah's hand, pointed to the woods and started to run. Leaves and branches slapped them in the face. They ran until Hannah couldn't run any more. She tripped, her fall jerking Magda to the ground as well.

"I can't!" she shouted.

Magda nodded.

Hannah watched Magda watching her. She closed her eyes, and sat motionless, trying to shut out the buzzing. She couldn't. It wouldn't stop. She placed her hands over her ears and pressed. It hurt. Her entire skull was filled with buzzing. Waves of it. She gritted her teeth and pressed harder. It felt like her head was going to burst. She opened her mouth wide and pressed harder. Then she heard a little pop. Then another. The buzzing began to subside. It was replaced by a distant whooshing. She listened. It was coming in waves. She realized it was her own breathing.

"I can hear my breathing!" she shouted, opening her eyes. "I can hear, I can hear!"

Magda smiled and held her palms over her chest.

"I can hear! I can hear!" Hannah shouted again and nodded. "Ow!" She laughed.

They reached out to each other and hugged for a long time. She felt free. Freedom was embracing. In the camp they embraced out of fear. They looked at each other in a way they hadn't in a long time. They looked at each other without having to worry about being yelled at or beaten. Here it was for the sheer pleasure of holding each other. It was exhilarating. They laughed and cried at the same time.

"How did you know about the fence?"

"I traded Anichka for the information. She told me that the road through the forest led to the border."

"What border?"

"The Czechoslovakian border. She told me that the Germans started to retreat from there."

Hannah stood up and slowly turned around. The green of pine trees, the blue of crocuses, the red of berries. It was almost too much to bear. She held her hands to her face and peeked through her fingers. The vivid colours of the world were making her dizzy. She leaned into a tree. That's what had been absent in the camp. There was no colour, just an ashen grey that filled the daily sky, body and the soul. Here, trees, shrubs, flowers; colour. Life.

"Tear it off!" Magda ordered.

Hannah looked at her sister in bewilderment. She didn't know what Magda was talking about. Maybe her hearing was not fully back, she thought.

"Tear it off," Magda repeated, pointing to her chest. "Now!"

She looked down and saw the yellow star. She had gotten so used to wearing it that she'd forgotten it was there. With animal ferocity, her sister clawed at her own chest. When it was finally off, she spat on it and threw it onto the ground. Hannah held hers in her palm, not quite sure what to do with it.

"Get rid of it," Magda said slapping it out of her hand. "Let's go."

The deeper into the forest they went, the more Hannah's senses awakened. She welcomed the feel of rough bark scraping against her skin, took deep gulps of the sharp scent of pine. She heard the chirping of birds, their flapping wings pounding in her ears as they took frightened flight. She wriggled her toes in the mud that oozed into her shoes. She licked the sticky sap on her fingers. She felt free. She had no idea how long this freedom would last. She didn't care. It was now. With the greed of a starving person, she devoured it.

19

The train slows down and then jerks to a halt. His mother's grip on him tightens. Tomi wants to cry out but remembering where he is, stops himself. He bites his lip. He hears the train's door clank open and the sound of boots. He stops breathing.

"Everybody off!" a voice calls out.

His father is still leaning against the door. Tomi hears people moving around outside the door, urging each other to hurry up. His father opens the door a crack.

"Pssst! Péter!"

"Sanyi!" Mr. Darvas cries out in surprise.

"Where are we?"

"Sopron."

"We're here," Tomi hears his mother whispers in his ear.

They wait for the wagon to completely empty. It takes him a few seconds to adjust to the light in the train. On the platform, he searches for Gabi and Emma-mama and Dezsö-papa.

"What happened to them?" he hears his father ask Mr. Darvas.

"Dezsö took a bad beating. They took him, Emma and Gabi, along with a bunch of others," Mr. Darvas says.

Tomi starts to cry. "Where's Gabi? I want Gabi."

"They'll be okay," his mother tries to reassure him. She tries to stroke his face but he slaps it away.

"I want Gabi! I want Gabi!"

"He'll be okay, I promise."

"Are they going to beat Gabi?"

"No. He's a brave little soldier. He'll be okay. We'll write to them."

"I want Gabi! I want Gabi!"

His father reaches down and lifts him. "He'll be all right. He's a brave boy. We'll see Gabi, Dezsö-Papa and Emma-mama very soon." He kisses him gently on the cheek.

"It hurts," he sobs and buries his head in his father shoulder. They're lying. He knows that he won't.

"Péter, why didn't they make *you* get off the train? *Your* visa application was rejected too."

"I put some money in our Identity Books. He took the bribe and let us stay."

"My husband knows how to do things right," Mrs. Darvas says in a way that makes Tomi want to spit at her.

"Where is Ernö?" his mother asks.

"He said he would meet us here," his father says.

"Sanyi! Sanyi!" a voice calls out from the far end of the station.

"Ernö! Thank God!"

"What happened? Why is the train so late?"

"The AVO stopped us."

"They also raided the station and rounded up most of the guides. I hid and just got back. Where is the other family?"

"The AVO."

"Then, let's go."

"Do you know Miska Kocsis?" Mr. Darvas asks.

"He was one of the guides arrested."

"What are we going to do?" Mrs. Darvas is beginning to get red in the face.

"Can you take us?" Mr. Darvas asks.

"I don't know you."

"I'll pay." Ernö looks at Mr. Darvas, his suitcases and Mrs. Darvas. He shakes his head. "You have too much," He points to the suitcases.

"Péter, make him!" Mrs. Darvas hisses.

"I'll pay whatever you ask."

Ernö shakes his head. Tomi feels happy.

"I'll vouch for them," Tomi's father says.

Ernö looks at them again. He looks to Sanyi. He nods.

His mother turns to Mrs. Darvas. "My husband knows how to do the right thing."

She takes Tomi's hand and follows Mr. Lakatos to the wagon that's hitched to a lamppost.

Mr. and Mrs. Darvas fall behind. Tomi can hear her panting as she's ordering Mr. Darvas to hurry and Mr. Lakatos to slow down.

Two other families are already aboard. His father lifts Tomi up onto the hay-strewn flatbed and helps his mother climb on before getting on himself. They crawl to the front and huddle in a corner behind the buckboard.

The horse snorts, raises its head and give its mane a shake. When Mr. Lakatos takes the reins and lightly taps the horse on its flank with the whip, it makes Tomi think of his grandfather. He feels sad that he didn't get to kiss his grandfather goodbye. He didn't get to say goodbye to Frog and Carrot and the blacksmiths and Gabi. He lost his friends and big brother. He cries quietly. He doesn't want anybody to hear him.

The wagon jerks forward and slowly wobbles towards the dark woods just beyond the train station. He wedges himself tightly between his parents and grabs their hands. And even though he feels them on either side, he feels scared and alone.

2 0

Sanyi's liberation arrived unannounced. There was no fierce battle, no explosions of shells, no rumbling tanks tearing down barbed wire fences, no blasting of trumpets, no waving of flags, no cheering of prisoners at the sight of liberating Allied soldiers. Sanyi's liberation came in absolute silence while he was asleep. It was announced by an absence of the morning martial music, by an absence of barking dogs, by an absence of guards banging open barrack doors, yelling at them to get up.

Out of habit, Sanyi rose and emerged from his bunk at the first light of day. What day he didn't know. He had lost track of days, months and years. He had a sense of hours but that was only because of the sundial one of his bunkmates had made, a stick stuck in the barren earth in front of their bunk. It was a small act of rebellion that gave them hope.

Like the others, he shuffled into his roll-call position and waited. And waited. But there was no roll call. Every morning, for however long he had been here, he and the others had been told when to wake, where to stand, where to go, when to eat, what to do and when to sleep. Now, standing here, guardless, he waited.

Sanyi thought he was dreaming. He looked up at the towers. They were empty; there were no guns trained on them. The camp gate was wide open. And there was the silence. He waited to wake up. As he stood there he also became aware of the others standing next to him also waiting. He became conscious of thinking. Were they part of his dream? Dreaming and thinking were alien acts. He hadn't done either for what seemed like forever.

No, it wasn't a dream. He was awake. He was thinking. What was going on? Was this the way they were going to be killed? Were the guards waiting for them to move before they came out of hiding and opened fire? He dared not move a muscle. He waited.

It seemed that everyone became conscious of their freedom simultaneously. The realization that there were really no guards, that the camp now belonged to them, came like a slap. Some skeletons sat down and started crying, some broke ranks and in a slow motion shuffled in all directions. Some headed toward the bakery, drawn by the heat and smell, emerging with loaves of bread in their arms, tearing off pieces and stuffing them in their mouths, or sitting on the ground rocking the loaves like babies. Some broke into the food pantry, that forbidden heaven, gorging themselves on whatever they found. Sanyi saw skeletons with raised handfuls of sugar, opening their mouths wide open and letting it cascade into their mouth. Others had fistfuls of lard that they were licking like ice cream. Men were drinking ladle after ladleful of milk. Sanyi watched them collapse in writhing agony. On the day of their liberation, he saw many die from being free.

Sanyi wandered around the camp aimlessly, not quite believing but still savouring his freedom. He wanted to be alone. He wanted to not see, hear or talk to anyone. He wanted silence. Something impossible a day before.

He entered the officers' mess. The abandoned room was set for breakfast. Immaculate white tablecloths draped the tables. On them, like attendant servants, all with the swastika insignia, all perfectly aligned, were plates, cups waiting to be filled, knives, forks waiting to carve into sausages, ham and fresh eggs, and napkins waiting to dab satisfied mouths. He reached for a cup but immediately stopped, afraid to touch it. He looked around, waiting to be slapped, but the dining hall was empty. Slowly he sat down, opened and carefully placed a napkin on his lap, reached out and lifted a sugar cube out of one of the pewter bowls. He put it between his lips, closed his eyes and sighed with pleasure as it dissolved. The rush of sweetness overwhelmed him. He held onto the table. When he had gathered his strength again, he stood up and slowly walked to the door.

He stood on the threshold and stared at the open camp gate. He closed his eyes, opened them, shut them and opened them again to see if the gate to the camp was still open. He experienced a lightness, a weightlessness. A soft breeze brushed against his face. It had a strange smell. He sniffed the air, trying to find its source. It was coming from his right. There he saw a high wooden fence with an open gate. It was through this gate that the officers disappeared at night. He followed the sweet familiar scent, trying to identify it. He stepped through the gate and it overwhelmed him. Lilac bushes in bloom. He closed his eyes and inhaled deeply. He felt himself smiling. He exhaled and opened his eyes. There were neatly kept lawns, swings and seesaws and colourfully painted houses. He wasn't sure where he was. It was a vaguely familiar world. He shuffled to the nearest house whose door was open as if it was waiting for him.

He found himself in a room with a large kitchen table in the centre that had on it a crystal glass vase filled with lilacs. Red-polka-dot curtains covered the windows. In one corner, next to another door, was a bookshelf and a record player. He stepped into the other room. He paused and sighed. At the far end was a large bed with a thick, fluffy duvet. He longed to be enveloped in its feathery softness. He caught sight of someone at the far end of the room. He squinted and saw a man with sunken cheeks, the skin on his bones drawn tight as a drum skin. The man's pyjama pants were too big, and like him, he was holding them up by the drawstrings. He too was moving toward the bed. Sanyi called out to him and the man called back. Sanyi raised his hand to warn him off, to tell him that this was his bed, but the man also waved to claim the bed. Sanyi made a run for it, just as the other man decided to do the same. When he finally realized he was looking into a mirror, he fainted.

Sanyi was floating on a fluffy cloud. Bright smiling faces began to drift by. "Hello," one of them said. It was a black face with bright eyes and shiny white teeth. Sanyi blinked, opened his eyes. The world was starting to take shape again. He touched his arms, his head. They didn't seem to belong to him. He was on a bed, on a soft mattress. A black man in uniform was holding a stethoscope against his chest and smiling at him.

"Hello. I help you. Okay?" Sanyi didn't understand the black man's gibberish. "I... help... you. HELP," he repeated slowly, H E L P, pointing at himself and then at Sanyi. What a strange dream. Oh, to dream, Sanyi thought to himself, as he fell into a deep sleep.

—

Two months after liberation, healthier, pounds heavier and louse free, Sanyi received identity papers from the Americans and was given permission to go home. He was no longer a number. He was Sándor Wolfstein again, though he was not sure who that was anymore. He and his fellow survivors from Békes, Péter Darvas and Israel Stern, started their journey home. The roads were dotted with men and women, usually in small groups, also leaving Hell. They stopped at farms along the way, begging for food and a place to sleep. Most farmers had very little food. A few shared but most were afraid and chased them off. Sometimes they stole. Sometimes they were allowed to sleep in the barns. Sometimes they huddled and slept in ditches.

It took them three weeks to reach Szabad. On the outskirts of Szabad was the labour camp, now abandoned, that Sanyi had been sent to work at before he was shipped to the concentration camp. It was here that he had first lost his freedom. But if he hadn't been assigned to the Szabad labour camp, he'd never have met Hannah.

In the early days of labour camp, conscripts were occasionally given leave to go home for the weekend. Békes was too far to walk, so he and others who stayed behind would go into Szabad on Friday nights, looking for mezuzahs. A Jew is commanded to welcome anyone who knocks at his door on a Sabbath night. It is a

Jew's duty to invite the stranger to sup with his family. Whenever they found one, one would knock while the others continued their search for other mezuzahs.

And so it was that Sanyi found himself knocking on Moses Schwartz's door on a Friday night.

"Who disturbs the peace?" a voice asked from the other side.

"I am Sándor Wolfstein, Zev Yakov ben Shmiel Yisroel, and I am from Békes. I am posted here at the labour camp and have come to welcome the Sabbath with you."

A man in his fifties opened the door. His face was covered in grey stubble and he held a stout staff in his hand. "I am Moses Schwartz, Moishe ben Zev Avrum, and I welcome you."

The aroma from the kitchen hit Sanyi so hard he could hardly stand. He held onto the back of a chair as he was introduced to Moses's wife Sara and their three daughters, Magda, Faigele and Hannah. He was struck by Hannah's beautiful face and shiny black shoulder-length hair. He took a deep breath. He inhaled the lavender fragrance of her hair and the fat flavoured steam of chicken soup, the sweetness of boiled carrots, and the meat-rich sholent. He fell in love. He came every Friday night until he was shipped to the concentration camp.

It was Hannah's house that Sanyi had in mind as the three liberated men finally reached Szabad late one evening. Walking down the familiar road he had walked those Friday nights, a lifetime ago it seemed, he wondered if any of them had survived—especially Hannah. He had thought of her while in camp but dared not dream of ever seeing her again. It was better not to.

Sanyi found the house. He stood in front of the door. The mezuzah was still there. He raised his fingers to his lips and hesitated before touching it lightly. It was the first mezuzah he had seen in two years. He took a deep breath and knocked.

There was no answer. He hesitated and knocked again, more forcefully. From somewhere inside, he heard movement.

"Who is it who disturbs the peace?"

Sanyi felt exhilaration at the sound of the voice. "I am Sándor Wolfstein, Zev Yankov ben Shmiel Yisroel!" he cried out.

The door opened quickly. There stood Moses, holding a lamp. He held it to Sanyi's gaunt face.

"Thank God! Thank God!" Moses said as they embraced. Both men began to cry.

2 1

"**P**apa! My fingers!"

"Oh. I'm sorry, my son." His father loosens up without letting go. He raises Tomi's hand to his lips, holds them there for a moment and kisses each of the fingers.

The cart has turned off onto a rutted road. Even though the horse is moving slowly, the wagon bounces up and down hard enough that Tomi thinks that he will fly out of the wagon like he almost had at his grandfather's.

He'd spent last summer with his grandfather, helping him take sacks of wheat to the mill. He remembered one morning, sitting on his grandfather's buckboard holding the reins while his grandfather went to open the gate. Without thinking he'd tapped the horse with the whip. The startled horse took off through the half-open gate, knocking it off its hinges. Tomi tried to pull the reins, but wasn't strong enough.

"Let go of the reins, Tomi! Let go of the reins!" his grandfather yelled, running after him. Tomi dropped the reins and grabbed the buckboard's seat, bouncing up and down as the horse trotted across the common, where it came to a stop, bent its head and began to graze. He saw his grandfather running towards him. Scared, he jumped off and ran and hid in the corn silo for the rest of the day. As he was being bounced about now, he thought how much he would like to be in that silo now.

They pull up in front of a farmhouse that looks like his grandfather's. By the light of the moon he sees that the roof is thatched with the same kind of long thin reeds. There is a large chimney right in the middle of it. The windows are small, shuttered and dark.

"Everybody line up against the wall," Mr. Lakatos whispers. Nobody moves.

"Quickly! Quickly," he hisses.

Still, no one moves. "Quickly, I said." His voice has a dangerous edge to it.

Sanyi jumps down, lifts Tomi out and reaches for Hannah. He looks at Ernö and then nods to Hannah. "It's okay," he says as they line up. His father stands in front of Tomi as if he is trying to shield him. The others follow and climb down from the wagon.

Mr. Lakatos knocks on the door—one strong thump follows three light taps. He repeats this twice. The door opens a crack. A low burning lamp illuminates his face. The person inside opens the door completely. Mr. Lakatos motions them in. An old woman, dressed in black from head to toe, stands by the door. Her lamp-lit face reminds Tomi of Mrs. János. Both resemble the witch in his old *Hansel and Gretel* book.

It's a small, low-ceilinged house. By the time everyone is inside, there is hardly any room. Some sit on chairs, others crouch and lean against the walls. Tomi and his parents huddle on a bench in the corner, next to the warm stove. Mr. and Mrs. Darvas sit on the daybed on the other side of it. Mr. Lakatos is the last one in.

"We're going to wait until there is better cloud cover and then I'm going to take you in two groups. The guards have been bribed, but make sure you have something extra just in case."

The old lady blows out the storm lamp, leaving only the low-burning oil lamp on the table, which casts an eerie orange glow over the room. The people become shadows and shapes. Frog's mother used to tell them stories of witches who lived in dark houses in dark forests; witches who turned people into shadows. These shadows were doomed to wander at night, looking for people who had no shadows. Shadowless people were afraid of the night. Once a shadow found such a person, usually a child who was afraid of the dark, it snuck up from behind and jumped on the child's back. It would sink its shadow fingers into the child's shoulders and slowly seep in and take over his soul until the little child became a shadow himself. And then the child would be doomed to wander the night searching for another shadowless person.

Tomi looks behind him. He can't see his shadow. He takes a deep breath and squishes himself against the wall.

Mr. Lakatos steps outside for a moment, comes back and nods. "We're ready to go." The old witch leaves the room and returns a minute later with a glass of pálinka. She hands it to Mr. Lakatos, who gulps it down and kisses her on the forehead. "Thank you, Mother. Okay, you and you and you, let's go!"

Tomi's family and Mr. and Mrs. Darvas will be the second group.

The old woman stands at the door, holding the lamp as the first group files out. She locks the door after them, turns to look at Tomi, his parents, Mr. and Mrs. Darvas, shakes her head and turns to the wall where there is a picture of a heart wrapped in thorns, like Emma-mama's rose thorns. There is blood dripping from the heart.

"What's that?"

"It's Jesus's heart."

"Why is it taken out from his body? Is that how he was killed?"

His mother gently places her palm over his lips. The old woman sighs as she gets down onto her knees, crosses herself and begins to pray. It's the first time he has seen anyone pray that way.

22

Hannah was sure that they were going in circles. Or worse. Maybe they were heading back to the factory. It seemed they had been wandering for hours. She was exhausted and ready to drop when Magda yelled, "It's the road."

A shaft of light split the forest. They ran toward it. It was narrow, nothing more than a well-worn wagon path. "We'll hide here until dark," she said, slipping back into the woods, just out of sight.

"Where are we going?" Hannah asked.

"Domazlice. Anichka said west. The sun is setting there, so we'll go that way. It's on the other side of the border."

"How far is the village?" Hannah asked.

"She said it was a few days."

Magda pulled out a sock from the pocket of her overalls. From it she took out a slice of bread. She tore off a morsel and handed it to her sister, then tore another for herself. "Here, our first meal of freedom."

"Then let's say a blessing." Hannah began, "Blessed are you God, King of the Universe, who brings forth bread from earth."

Magda did not reply with the usual Amen. "I'm done with Him," she said. "You should be too. No matter what happens, from now on, good or bad, it's my own doing."

"But Magda, what about Mama and Faigele? We can't forget."

"Believe me, I never will. I don't need Him to remind me of what happened. They died because of Him. Don't you forget it!

And don't forget who carried out His orders. Not just the Nazis but those who stood in their doorways and did nothing. Those good neighbours. Those good Christians. And they'll do it again. Never trust them again. Remember, the only good *goyim* is a dead *goyim*." Magda took a vicious bite and put the rest of the slice back into the sock and tucked the sock into her overalls. They sat in silence in the thicket and waited for night to fall.

Magda was right. Only family mattered. There is only family. And right now that's just us, Hannah thought to herself. Just us. She began to cry.

They had been walking for two nights. The bread was gone and there wasn't much to scrounge for in the woods. Sometimes they came across wild asparagus and chickweed, but they were scarce, and the berries weren't quite ripe yet. But after their time in the camps, they were used to hunger. They knew how to not eat. They had survived on less.

Day was coming on. Hannah sat and leaned against a tree and drifted off to sleep. She dreamt of chimneys. They had stork nests on them and they were filled with baby storks whose hungry beaks reached for the sky. She saw smoke rise through them and then suddenly flames burst out of the nests. The sky became red as the flames rose up to the heavens, mushroomed out and turned into grey snowflakes that began to fall on her. She felt like she was being choked. She tried to cover her mouth and gasped awake to falling rain. It was dark. Hannah heard something, and looked around but couldn't see Magda. She heard another sound nearby. A roaming pack of wolves? Or worse, Germans? Perhaps partisans. Rumours had it that they were just as bad.

"Magda!" she shouted.

Magda appeared. "Quiet. Time to go."

"Oh God, you scared me."

"This way."

They set out under the half-moon, sticking close enough to the woods to run for cover if they needed to. They followed the muddy, rutted track as it wound its way to somewhere. The mud seeped into her laceless, holey shoes and the rain beat down on her. She rubbed her head. She had forgotten that she had no hair. The stubbles prickled under her touch. She caressed them.

Even though they had rested, Hannah felt as though she had been walking for years. The first thrill of freedom had worn off and now she just wanted to be somewhere. She thought of home and wondered what it would be like to be there. Without realizing it, she began singing a song she had learned in camp.

Oh if I survive Dear Lord
Oh if I return home again
Will I have my dear father to embrace?
Oh if I somehow survive this hell
Will there be someone to tell?
Will there be someone to tell?
Dear Lord, will there be someone to tell?

As the first light of day broke through the dark, the rain began to let up. A rooster crowed nearby.

Magda took Hannah's arm. "Quick! This way."

They ran into the woods and crouched behind some bushes. When Magda felt it was safe, they crept slowly to the edge of the woods. A clearing, like the commons in Szabad, separated the woods from a village of thatched houses with tall chimneys. They saw wafting plumes of morning smoke. Hannah thought of her mother's thick porridge, warm milk and slices of fresh bread.

"I'm hungry."

Magda motioned her to be quiet. Kneeling, they watched four girls, about their age, as they herded geese toward the clearing. The girls stopped a short distance from where Magda and Hannah were hiding and sat down in a circle under a large maple. The geese honked as they wandered about, pecking at the ground for loose grain and grazing on the new spring grass. A collie dashed back and forth, yapping, keeping the geese from wandering into the woods.

"Maybe we should ask them for food," Hannah said.

"I don't trust them."

"They're women."

"So?"

"I trust women."

"I don't. There were women guards in the camp. If they're not Jewish, I don't trust them," Magda said.

"I'm hungry," Hannah repeated, and as if in a trance, stood and began walking.

"No!" Magda hissed and hurried after her. The dog started barking. One of the women looked up and pointed at them. When they were close, Magda and Hannah stopped. The women stared at each other. "Nazdar," Magda said. It was all the Czechoslovakian she knew.

The eldest nodded. "Nazdar."

"Hungarian. Do you speak Hungarian?" Magda asked in Hungarian.

The woman shrugged her shoulders.

"Sprechen Sie Deutsch?" asked Hannah.

The young woman spat. "Ja."

With their Yiddish and what they had learned in camp, Hannah and Magda knew enough German to get by.

"We are Hungarians," explained Magda. "We worked in factory and then boom-boom." She made airplane wings with her arms.

The women continued to stare at them.

"Zidovske?" one of the girls asked, pointing to the outline where the star had been sewn onto Magda's overalls.

Magda looked down at her chest, hesitated and then nodded. No one said anything, no one moved.

"Anichka Gutmann," Magda said.

The oldest smiled. "Anichka, Anichka Gutman," she repeated. "Alive?" she asked in German.

"Yes," Magda replied.

The woman crossed herself, put her hands together and looked up to the sky and smiled. The others followed suit. She signalled Hannah and Magda to come closer. The woman reached into her small wicker basket and offered them a slice of bread. Wide-eyed, they stared at the fresh, golden-crusted bread.

"Eat," she said, making a munching sound with her mouth.

"Thank you." Magda took the bread, tore it in half and offered it to Hannah.

"No. No," the woman said, shaking her head. She took out a second piece of bread and offered it to Hannah. "Sit." She patted the ground beside her.

The other two women reached into their baskets and offered green peppers, shallots, carrots, cheese and more bread. In silence they watched Magda and Hannah as they nibbled at the food, trying to make it last forever.

The roar of engines shook the air, followed by a cloud of dust. It came from the village. Everyone turned to look. A motorcycle with a sidecar was heading toward them. Trucks filled with German soldiers rumbled closely behind.

Hannah and Magda leapt up and started to run back toward the woods. "No! No!" the oldest yelled and said something in Czechoslovakian. One of the other girls grabbed Magda and held her firmly by the wrists. Hannah rushed at the woman, trying to free Magda. But she was stronger. She shouted something to the others and they grabbed Hannah and pushed her to the ground. One of them took off her head scarf and wrapped it around Hannah's head. Another took hers off and gave it to Magda and pointed to her head. She signalled for them to be quiet. Then the four women stood in front of Hannah and Magda.

The approaching motorcycle slowed down. The officer in the sidecar pointed to the women and shouted at the driver to stop. The women stared back. Hannah was afraid to breathe. The officer nodded. "You can have your country back." He saluted with his riding crop and tapped the driver. They roared off.

"Nazis," the woman spat. The others did the same. They turned to face the sisters.

"Nazis!" repeated Hannah and Magda. They spat.

Once the convoy disappeared into the forest, the women fell to their knees, crossed themselves and prayed. Hannah and Magda also knelt, and ate.

2 3

A loud knock wakes Tomi. He had been dreaming of playing with Gabi. He was taking shots on goal, but before any of them could reach Gabi the balls exploded. There were tanks on the Golden Green firing at the balls. He couldn't get any of his shots through. Gabi was standing in front of the net waving his arms at him.

The loud knock is followed by three light taps, and silence. Then the knocks are repeated. The old lady groans as she gets off her knees and goes to unlock the door.

"Everything went well. There were no border guards. They're on their way."

"God be praised," the old lady says and crosses herself. She disappears into the pantry and returns with another glass of pálinka. Mr. Lakatos lifts it to his lips, but stops. "Mother, bring two more glasses, please." He fills them and gives one to Tomi's mother and the other to his father. They lift their glasses. "Le Kaim," Mr. Lakatos says, drinking it down in one gulp.

"La Chaim," his father and mother reply. His father takes a sip, then passes it to Tomi. He sips and then passes it back to his father, who passes it to Mr. Darvas. His mother passes hers to Mrs. Darvas.

"To life," they say together.

Mr. Lakatos kisses his mother on her forehead and slaps his palms together. "It's time."

Following his parents to the door, Tomi pats his schoolbag to make sure his soccer ball is safely inside. He glances behind him and sees his shadow. A warmth spreads through him.

—

They walk toward the far end of the yard where the woods begin.

"Single file," Mr. Lakatos says, before leading them along the narrow path.

Tomi, who is between his parents, keeps turning around to make sure that his mother is still behind him. Mrs. Darvas trails behind her, breathing heavily, followed Mr. Darvas.

"Slow down. Slow down," Mrs. Darvas pleads.

"Shush," Tomi's mother says quietly and reaches back to take her hand.

The moon, hidden behind the clouds, occasionally peeks out. Tomi is tired but excited. And even if it's kind of scary to be in the woods so late, he isn't afraid because he drank the pálinka, he is a member of a warrior tribe and he has his shadow. And also, he has decided not to be afraid.

The moon, hidden behind clouds, occasionally peeks out. In the dark, it is hard to see anything, especially the path. Branches like skeleton's fingers scrape across his puffed face and sore arm. Tomi slaps at them.

His father leans down to pick him up. "No," he says, though he would like to tuck his head into his father's neck and feel his warm breath. "No," he says again. "I drank pálinka. I'm grown-up now."

"Yes. Yes, you are. Just keep your hands in front of you like this," his father says and takes his hands and crosses them in front of his face to show him how.

"Stop!" Mr. Lakatos orders. "This is the end of the woods. Do you see that light?" He points into the distance. "That's the village of Schattendorf. It's in Austria. The people lit up the church tower there as a beacon for you. Just head toward it in a straight line and once you are there, you'll be free."

The light looks like a flickering, shining star.

"About half a kilometre from here, you'll come to a small stream. It's the run-off from Lake Fertö. It's not deep this time of year and there are logs strewn across it. About fifty metres or so on the other side of it is a railroad embankment. Don't worry, there's only one freight train a night, but that won't be for at least another hour, if it comes at all. After that, you walk through some scrub brush, but not much. The area is rarely patrolled, and these days, probably not at all. But have your bribe ready, just in case. After that, you'll be on the Hungarian side of No Man's Land. It's only about a kilometre from there to the church in Schattendorf. May God be with you."

No Man's Land. What kind of place is No Man's Land? Tomi wonders. Why aren't there men there? It sounds like a bad place. Why do they have to go there?

"I thought you were going to lead us across No Man's Land," Mr. Darvas says.

"We paid you good money to get us safely across, not to abandon us in the middle of nowhere," Mrs. Darvas shouts.

"Be quiet, madam! I said I would go to the edge with you. I didn't ask you to come along. You begged me. You want to go back? I will give you back your money. This is where I leave you."

Mr. Lakatos turns to Tomi's father. "Since the other family didn't make it, this is yours now," he says as they shake hands.

Tomi's father nods.

Mr. Lakatos turns and disappears into the woods.

"We paid him good money. Péter, why didn't you do something?"

"That's enough, Ágnes! Don't talk to me like that."

Mrs. Darvas gasps.

"We're on our own now," his father says.

"Then, let's go," his mother says, taking Tomi's hand. Without looking back, she begins walking toward the light.

———

The clouds have thinned and now the moon is shining down on them. There are no logs across the water.

"Now what?" says Mrs. Darvas. "He was lying. Why didn't you wait to pay him only when he took us to No Man's Land?"

"We'll walk upstream," Tomi's father snaps. "You can go the other way if you want." He sets off, Tomi and his mother following. He looks back and sees Mr. and Mrs. Darvas not moving, looking at each other, and then Mr. Darvas bends down, puts the cord over his head, lifts the suitcases and they follow.

"It must be the other way," Mr. Darvas says when they stop for a rest.

"I'm not wasting any more time looking. We're crossing here." His father points to some protruding boulders.

"I'm not getting wet. Péter, do something!"

Tomi's father shrugs off his leather coat and sits on it. He removes his shoes and socks, tucks the socks into the shoes, ties the laces together and hangs them around his neck, rolls his pant legs up to his knees and stands up. His mother does the same.

"Ayyyyy," his father hisses as he steps into the stream. "Pass me my coat." He slings it over his shoulder. "Tomi, come here," he says holding out his arms and picking him up. "Now you're going to hold Mama's coat. Okay?"

Tomi nods. "Hannah, pass him your coat. Now, can you guard that?"

Tomi nods again and clasps it tightly against his chest. He leans against his father's neck. I drank pálinka. I'm a Cohen, he tells himself again.

His father extends his free hand to his mother, takes a deep breath and starts to wade further and deeper. Tomi watches the water rise with each slow and careful step that his father takes. He looks back over his father's shoulder and sees that the water is above his mother's thighs. He can see her face in the moonlight. She is taking sharp hissing breaths through her tightly pursed lips. He feels himself being lifted and then placed down on the bank. Tomi watches his father reach back and help his mother up onto the shore. Just like a knight, Tomi thinks.

Mr. and Mrs. Darvas are still on the other side, arguing.

"I am not crossing that way," Mrs. Darvas says.

"I'll come back for you."

Mr. Darvas, who is smaller and fatter than Tomi's father, takes off his coat but leaves his shoes on. He wobbles from side to side as he takes the first steps, waddling like a goose. He tries to keep the suitcases above water but they're too heavy. He's almost halfway across the stream when he slips, loses his balance, shouts and disappears underwater.

"Péter!" Mrs. Darvas screams.

"Mr. Darvas," Tomi shouts at the same time. His father, who is drying his feet, sees a hand reaching up from below the water. He splashes back into the stream.

"Péter! Péter!" his father is shouting, trying to grab Mr. Darvas' flailing hand. He can't. He reaches into the stream and grabs a clumpful of his hair and pulls but he can't lift him. "The cord is around his neck! I can't pull him up!"

"Péter! Péter! Save him!" Mrs. Darvas cries.

His mother wades back into the water and grabs Mr. Darvas by the shoulder and they pull, but even together they can't budge him.

"Sanyi, hold his head," Hannah shouts as she takes out her knife. She plunges it into the water and suddenly Mr. Darvas' head bobs up.

They start to drag him toward the shore. Tomi grabs the back of Mr. Darvas's collar and helps to pull him up, as Mr. Darvas starts coughing and spitting water.

"The suitcases. The suitcases!" Mrs. Darvas shouts from across the water.

"Shut up! Take off your coats and cross over," Tomi's mother calls out to her.

"I can't. I can't," she wails.

"Hurry up! Do it!"

"I can't! I can't."

"Come, Ágnes. It's not deep."

"No! No!"

Mr. Darvas gets to his feet and without a word steps back into the water and wades back to the other shore. When he emerges, he embraces his wife. She puts her head on his shoulder and sobs.

Mr. Darvas looks back across the stream. He shakes his head and waves them on.

His father hesitates.

"Let's go." His mother takes Tomi's hand and begins walking.

2 4

The train track, just as Mr. Lakatos said, isn't far from the stream. But the embankments are steep. They need to descend, cross the track, and get up the embankment on the other side.

"How are we going to get down?" His mother sounds tired.

"Let's slide!"

His parents look at him and smile. "Let's," his father says and the three join hands.

Like children sliding at the park, he and his parents let out a spontaneous "Wheeee!"

Seconds later, they are standing on the tracks laughing. He hasn't seen his parents like this in a long time. It's like a weight has been lifted off them. It's like they're kids. He's made them happy. He's happy. Tomi stands on one of the shiny tracks with his arms out, like a high-wire acrobat on a circus tightrope.

"The track is vibrating," Tomi says.

"Train!" Hannah cries, snatching Tomi. "Take him on your back, Sanyi. Hold on to Papa, Tomi!" Now they can hear the rumble of the approaching train.

"Hold on tight!" she shouts as his father starts clawing his way up the gravel embankment. His father scrambles for a foothold, dislodging pebbles and dirt as he climbs, some of it raining onto his mother as she clambers up behind them. The rumble grows louder. Sanyi is slipping and pushing her down.

"Sanyi, don't move!" she screams. The train is upon them. They all lie still halfway up, pressed against the embankment. Hannah is pushing and holding Sanyi's heel at the same time.

Tomi has the sensation that the vibration and pressure from the train is going to crush him into his father, making them one body. His ears pound and his body shakes as the train thunders by for what seems like forever.

"Hannah. Are you okay?" his father shouts once the rumble dies away and silence returns.

He looks over his shoulder. She's flattened against the embankment. "Are you okay?" he shouts again.

"Yes!" she calls back.

His father starts to claw his way up the embankment. When he reaches the top, he turns quickly and Tomi rolls off him. His father reaches down to pull up his mother. He embraces her and hugs her tight. She is shaking. "Oh God. Oh God," he keeps repeating.

Tomi starts to get up.

"Halt!"

Tomi freezes.

"Hands up!" the voice orders. "Stand up! Turn around!"

Slowly, they stand, raise their hands and turn around. A shadowy figure, outlined by the moon, is aiming a rifle at them. A light snow is falling. The shadow comes closer. It's a soldier. He's young, probably no older than Fire.

"Soz, you think you're gonnascape? Gonna leave the Motherland?" The soldier's voice is loud, but his speech is slurred.

"Soldier Sir, with your permission, I have something for you," his father says pointing to his coat pocket.

"Whaz dat?" the young guard is waving the rifle back and forth at them.

"A wonderful bottle of homemade pálinka."

Tomi watches his father move away from him. He feels his father is abandoning him.

The soldier stares at his father. "Lezsee."

"It's the finest quality," his father says as he takes another step, opens his coat and reaches slowly into his pocket. "You know what they say, a glass of pálinka is good medicine, but a bottle is the whole remedy."

"Give it over," the soldier orders, moving closer.

"Papa," Tomi shouts as the young soldier steps forward and reaches for the bottle. The soldier turns toward Tomi, stumbles and loses his balance. The rifle goes off. He falls, face down, into the frozen hard ground.

A bright flash explodes in front of Tomi's eyes. He feels a searing pain and falls to his knees. He grabs his head in his hands and before everything goes black, he sees his mother leap like a panther onto the soldier's back and lifts his head up by his hair. Her knife flashes in the moonlight. She growls, "Never again!"

PRONUNCIATION GUIDE

Aranyi:	A-ra-nyee ('ny' as in 'new')
Árpád:	The Á is the "ah" you say for the doctor
Bozsik:	Bo-zs ik ('zs' as the 's' in leisure)
Budai:	Boo-da-ee
Budapest:	Boo-da-pesht
Buzansky:	Boo-zan-ski
Chaider:	Hey-der
Cibor:	Tsi-bore
Darvas:	Dar-wash
Dezsö:	Deh-zsö ('zs' as the 's' in leisure, 'ö' as the 'e' in her)
Dohany:	Doh-hany ('ny' as in 'new')
Fekete:	Feh-ke-teh ('ke' as in 'can')
Ferenc:	Fe-renc ('c' as in 'tsar')
Fertö:	Fer-tö ('ö' as the 'e' in 'her')
Földember:	Föld-ember (the 'ö' as the 'e' in 'her' and 'ember' as in 'September')
Gabi:	Ga-bee ('ga' as in 'gaga,' baby talk) (diminutive of Gábor)
Gábor:	Gá-bore ('ga' as in 'gaga' baby talk)
Gombás:	Gom-básh ('ásh' as in 'pasha')
Grosics:	Gro-shi-ch ('ch' as in 'Chicago')
Gyuri:	Jew-ree
Hajdúbékes:	Hie-do-bay-késh
Hajdúdobos:	Hie-do-doe-bosh
Hajdúbszabad:	Hie-do-sa-bawd
Hidegkuti:	He-degg-ku-tee
Honvéd:	Hon-vade
Huszár:	Hu-sar ('sz' as in 'Sam')
Imi:	Eee-me (diminutive of Imre)
Imre:	Eem-reh

Jóska:	Yo-sh-ka
Kistarcsa:	Quiche-tar-cha
Kocsis:	Ko-chish
Laci:	La-tsi (diminutive for Lászlo)
Lantos:	Lan-tosh
Lászlo:	La-s-lo
Lorant:	Lo-rant
Mangalica:	Mahn-ga-lee-tsa
Miska:	Mish-ka
Nemecsek:	Ne-meh-check
Pálinka:	Pal-lin-ka ('pal' as in 'pal')
Pogácsa:	Po-ga-cha ('ga' as in baby talk 'gaga')
Puskás:	Push-kásh
Rákóci:	Rah-ko-tsi ('rah' as in 'Raj')
Rákosi:	Rah-ko-shee ('rah' as in 'Raj')
Ruskie:	Roo-skee (diminutive and derogatory term for a Russian)
Sándor:	Shan-dor
Sanyi:	Sha-nyee (diminutive for Sándor)
Shofar:	Sho-far
Szeles:	Ce-lesh ('c' as in 'celery')
Tamás:	Ta-mash (as in 'mash')
Tibor:	Tee-bore
Tomi:	Toe-mee (diminutive for Tamás)
Toth:	Tote
Tzitit:	Tsi-tsit
Yarmulke:	Yar-mul-ka
Zakarias:	Za-ka-ree-ash
Zoli:	Zo-lee (diminutive for Zoltán)

AFTERWORD

Like most first works of fiction, *Never, Again* contains elements of my life and experiences. I was about Tomi's age at the time of the 1956 Uprising, my parents are Holocaust survivors, and we had some of the "adventures" I built the story around. However, *Never, Again* is fiction and should be read as such.

Much has changed in the intervening sixty years in Hungary. Communist rule has ended and, technically, Hungary is a democracy. Even so, the bias against Jews and Roma has never entirely disappeared and Hungary's dark underbelly is becoming increasingly visible. Xenophobic nationalism with all its dark tentacles is on the rise again.

According to Holocaust historian Raul Hilberg, the phrase "Never Again" first appeared on handmade signs put up by inmates at Buchenwald in April, 1945, shortly after the camp was liberated by U.S. forces. "Never Again" became the call of remembrance, a declaration and defiance of survivors and the world. Since then, however, the phrase has been used after each subsequent genocide, and "Never, Again" has become a declaration of the world's failure to prevent the horror from being repeated.

ABOUT THE AUTHOR

The son of Holocaust survivors, Endre Farkas was born in Hajdunánás, Hungary. He escaped with his parents during the 1956 Hungarian Uprising and settled in Montreal. A poet, playwright and now novelist, Farkas has published nine books of poetry — including *Murders in the Welcome Café, Romantic at Heart & Other Faults, How To,* and *Quotidian Fever, New and Selected Poems,* and has had two plays produced — *Haunted House,* which is based on the life and work of the poet A.M. Klein, and *Surviving Wor(l)ds,* an adaptation of his book of poems *Surviving Words.* He collaborated with poet Carolyn Marie Souaid on the video poem *Blood is Blood,* which won first prize at The Berlin International Poetry Film Festival in 2012. Farkas has given readings throughout Canada, USA, Europe and Latin America. He is also the two-time regional winner of the CBC Poetry Face-Off competition. His poems have been translated into French, Spanish, Hungarian, Italian, Slovenian and Turkish.